# BIG 'N BURLY BOX SET 3

## BIG & BURLY

### REINA TORRES

Mahalo—
Angelia

Aloha
Reina
Torres

Copyright © 2023 by Reina Torres

All rights reserved.

No part of this book may be reproduced in any form or by any electronic or mechanical means, including information storage and retrieval systems, without written permission from the author, except for the use of brief quotations in a book review.

AI RESTRICTION: The author expressly prohibits any entity from using any part of this publication, including text and graphics, for purposes of training artificial intelligence (AI) technologies to generate text or graphics, including without limitation technologies that are capable of generating works in the same style or genre as this publication. The author reserves all rights to license uses of his work for generative AI training and development of machine learning language models.

The CONTENT of this book and its GRAPHICS are 100% Human Generated.

Graphic editing by: Golden Czermak of Furious Fotog

Cover Template by: Elle Christensen; Clover Book Designs

Logo Design by: Sweet 'n Spicy Designs

# BOSSED BY THE DAD BOD

Doyle Crane is the man people look to for reassurance. He's a rock. The people who work for him. The people who live in town. His teenage daughter even laughs at his jokes... *once in a while.* He keeps himself busy, so he won't think about what he's missing. What's even worse is he's found her. New in town, making a new life for herself. What he wouldn't do to get his hands on her, but he's afraid he'll scare her away. She's just too sweet to be bossed around by the likes of him.

Shelby Akers is new in town and new to love, but that didn't stop her from falling for Doyle Crane the first day she met him. It wasn't love at first sight when he helped pull her car out of the mud or when he shook his head at how she was shivering in the rain, but it most certainly was when he took off his coat, wrapped it around her body and gave her a heated appraising look and muttered, "Someone needs to take care of you, Shelby."

Doyle knows he's too bossy to even think of getting close to Shelby. She needed a nice, easy-going guy who could be gentle with her, someone who wasn't him.

That all changed when her boss put her in danger.

He went from hands-off, seemingly unaffected Doyle to demanding, bossy-as-fu...dge, *hands-all-over* protector. Shelby couldn't be happier.

# CLAIMED BY THE DAD BOD

*She wanted to stand on her own two feet*
*He knew she needed to be swept off them every once in a while*

Everything Nathaniel Sterling had in his life he worked for. He had friends and employees who he cared about, but no one to come home to. He had a friend with benefits. No, scratch that. She wasn't all that friendly and lately the benefits... weren't all that great either.

Who would've guessed that he'd meet the love of his life over a box full of neon-bright condoms?

Evelyn Connors has had a string of bad luck since she moved away from Heaven, Oklahoma. Her latest job is for a horrible jerk of a boss, and she manages to white-knuckle her way through every shift. Who knew that a man would walk in one night and steal her breath with his kindness and the easy way they could talk to each other.

Eve had no idea that the spark she felt with Nathaniel would come back to burn her. The woman he came in with wasn't ready to let Nathaniel go and she didn't care who got in the way of her plan to claw him back.

Nathaniel knows who he wants. Eve.
He just needs to show her that forever can start with a moment, and he'll pull out all the stops to do it. Eve is going to find out that she's been claimed. And Nathaniel is playing for keeps.

# WATCHED BY THE DAD BOD

**Ronan and Poppy are next-door neighbors who can't help but watch each other when they think the other isn't looking. In this case, cupid isn't blind, but he's definitely got great aim.**

Ronan Duncan has been a Private Investigator for years, and he's nearly burnt out. These days the only person he wants to watch is Poppy Tanner, the woman who owns the coffee shop in the next building. He finds himself scheduling his work around her schedule just to keep an eye on her.

Poppy Tanner is tired of being watched. She went on two abysmal dates and now Grant won't take no for an answer, calling and leaving her gifts that make his obsession crystal clear. He wants her or he'll make sure that no one else can have her.

One night, the motion sensor Ronan set up to keep her safe blares an alarm and before he knows what's going on, he's leaping across their balconies to her apartment to save her life.

Now he wants forever, but how will Poppy react to having

Ronan love and cherish her for the rest of their lives instead of being Watched by the Dad Bod?

# INKED BY THE DAD BOD

**It's hard to predict what brings two people together.**

Lily and Vincent are two who find themselves drawn together with the inevitable pull of magnetism. Are they a pair of opposites drawn together in a perfect match, or are they too much alike to be together?

Vincent Kane never really considered himself a tattoo artist. He found himself drawn to the craft for its own merits. The artistry was a product of his mind, his building business to his hard work and determination.

After a few years as a partner in their current shop, Vincent finds himself disillusioned by his partner and inextricably drawn to his partner's apprentice. How will he straighten the tangle he's made of his life? Especially when he can't seem to keep his thoughts off of his partner's gorgeous apprentice.

Lily Weber found a position as an apprentice at Ink Envy, but she's worried that she's out of her element. Tattoo artist 'Hannibal' Baldwin is talented, but he also makes her skin crawl.

He doesn't seem to be as interested in helping her develop the skills of her hands as he wants to get his hands on her. If only he was like this partner, Vincent. Lily can't keep her mind off of the other artist who headlines the shop. He features in her dreams both night and day.

Life seems to throw them together over and over, but there's a tall and oh-so-handsy obstacle between them. What will it take for Vincent and Lily to find that they can create more than art? They could create a lifetime of beauty... together?

Lily may find herself Inked by the Dad Bod.

# HIDDEN BY THE DAD BOD

# HIDDEN BY THE DAD BOD

Amos Kane

He was forced to retire early as a U.S. Marshal when he lost a witness and nearly his life. Since that time, he's been happy, well 'relatively' happy to hunker down in the woods by his lonesome.

No one needs to deal with his anger and disappointment.

A WITSEC marshal shows up and leaves a witness on his doorstep before speeding off to catch a suspect.

He wasn't even given the chance to say no and try as hard as he can to keep his distance, he finds himself drawn to her. Damn it.

April Reynolds

April's life was simple and easy until that morning. Going through the motions until she's a witness to a double murder.

Shoved into a car, a federal agent takes her into the woods and drops her off at a cabin owned by the grumpiest man she'd ever seen.

Too bad he was also the most attractive man she'd ever met. Shoot and double shoot.

April isn't used to hiding away from the world. She's a people person, but the cabin tucked away in the woods and its owner have their own charm. She's just not sure things will work out when she's Hidden by the Dad Bod

# CHAPTER ONE

There's something simply satisfying about working with animals. They give you what you give to them. You show love and a generosity of spirit and they give it back to you. Well... except for Huskies.

Oh, don't get her wrong. She loves the little hellions, but they're a bit on the dramatic side.

Okay. They're divas.

But they're beautiful divas.

And April Reynolds loves all the pups. She has since she was a child and dreamed of having a dog of her own. That didn't happen, and when she graduated high school, she didn't decide to go to college. She went straight to work.

As a dog walker.

Then a dog groomer.

And now, well... she did a bit of both.

Princess was a husky. And Princess did everything under the sun to remind April of that every time they had their monthly sessions.

Princess' dog mom was Leora Helms a wealthy woman and dog dad was a bank executive. She was pretty sure that his name was Frank or Ed or something along those lines. She'd never met him, so it didn't matter much.

Neither did the fact that Leora didn't seem to know that Princess was a boy. The couple of times that she'd brought it up to Leora, the woman just waved it away. "Do you have any idea how many things we have with Princess' name on it? What does it matter?"

And it didn't matter, not to April really.

Princess was pampered. He ate well. He had a whole room to himself with toys and a bed that any princess, human or animal, would find gorgeous and yes, over the top.

When she arrived at the security gate, April spoke into the security device at the front and unlike the other times that she'd arrived to groom Princess, the security guard took almost a minute to answer her greeting.

"Sorry. Who are you?"

"Uh, I'm April Reynolds? I groom Princess?"

"Oh. Sure. Sorry about that."

As the massive gate swung open, April smiled and leaned into the security screen. "You guys okay in there? You sound a little... tense."

"No. Sorry, miss. We have a lot going on today. Mister Helm is still on the property."

"Oh? Is it a bank holiday?" The gates seemed a little sluggish. "Does that mean I finally get to meet the man?"

"Do... do you want to?"

"No." She shifted in her seat. "It was just a thought. I've got my hands full with Princess."

"Have a good day, miss."

So, not much for conversation? She shrugged. It wasn't what she was there for, anyway.

With the gates opened enough to get her red and white

Kei Mini Van through, she puttered off, looking forward to her dramatic customer.

When she arrived at the back door, April pushed the doorbell and waited. Again, it took a little more time than it normally did, but April didn't mind. She left a good window of time in her schedule for Princess. As gorgeous as the husky was, he was a handful.

Two, really.

So she padded the time in her schedule so that the next dog she was going to see wasn't until later. If she had time after her appointment with Princess, she'd take a lunch break at a park somewhere, sitting in the open side doorway of her van and enjoying the fresh air and scenery.

And waiting outside the back door wasn't a hardship. The grounds on the estate were immaculate and changed with the seasons.

It was hard to imagine how much a service like that would cost, but it wasn't something that she dwelled on for long. She turned back to smile at her little red and white van with the PRETTY PUPPY Mobile Grooming Service logo and felt a spike of pride bubble up inside her chest.

She was her own business owner and good at what she did. What more could she want?

The door opened before she could push the doorbell button again and she was startled to see Leora Helm herself open the door.

The normally elegant woman had pieces of hair straggling from her updo and she held up a finger at April to give her a moment.

April took a step to the side and leaned against the half wall to the side of the door.

Working with squirming dogs, some of them heavier than

she was, gave her back a workout. When she could rest her back she did, eagerly.

Princess, she knew, was a wiggler of the highest order.

And a yelper.

A whiner.

A little scamp that was almost half her weight.

"Okay, fine. Just hurry."

Leora poked her finger at the screen of her phone like it had personally done her wrong. With that done, she turned to look at April. "I thought I'd called you."

April's brow furrowed and she pulled her phone out of her overall's bib pocket. "Nope. No calls, Missus Helm. I'm here to groom Princess."

She was sure to give the other woman an eager smile. Leora wasn't the happiest of women on any day, but on this day she looked particularly harried.

"That's why I called you. You can't groom her today."

April didn't argue with the other woman, she liked the job grooming Princess whether or not the dog was a girl, and so she wasn't going to contradict a woman who paid her a very nice tip when she was done. That tip alone helped pay for gas to all of her appointments for a couple of weeks.

"I'm sorry. It must be my cell service. Would you like me to come back on another day?"

She was already holding her phone, so April switched apps to her calendar. "I'll be happy to make time for Princess any day."

"I don't want you here today, okay?"

Leora was leaning on the doorframe with one hand, her makeup looked a little smudged, and her eyes a little bright."

"Missus Helm, are you feeling okay? May I call someone for you?"

"Look!" She huffed out a breath and her nostrils flared

open. For once, since she'd known the woman, April felt like Leora was close to losing her temper. "I said to go! It would have been better if you didn't come today. Now, please leave."

April's gaze moved over her face and the more she looked, the more concerned she became.

Sure, she could leave. Mrs. Helm had asked her to go.

Still, April didn't feel good about leaving Mrs. Helm if she didn't feel good.

April knew that when she was sick, she forgot to do the simplest things for herself.

She could have a medicine chest full of medication perfectly suited to make her feel better, but April knew she lost her head a little bit when she was sick and couldn't do more than just lay there, blinking up at the ceiling, unless someone got her up and took her to the doctor or something similar.

Maybe Mrs. Helm was the same.

"I thought I could help. If Nancy's not here-"

Leora's coloring suddenly disappeared. Her normally elegant makeup looked as if it was painted over a plain white canvas.

"Please, just go."

"Okay."

There was something different in Mrs. Helm's voice.

Something cold.

Something desperate.

Okay.

Even if Nancy had the day off, there had to be at least half a dozen servants in the mansion on any given day. Mrs. Helm would be well cared for.

"Sorry to bother you, ma'am. Please call me later when you want to resch-"

"This is taking too long."

Leora staggered sideways as something touched the side of her head.

Oh, god.

It was a gun. Or rather, the barrel of one.

And she kept moving as more of the gun came into view. The gun and the man holding it.

"And who might you be?"

He had a look better suited to a Soap Opera villain than a criminal.

Well, it wasn't like she would know, really. The only villains she'd actually had any experience with were on TV or in the movies, but this man...

This man she knew was evil.

He pulled on a part of the gun he was holding and she heard something metal connect with metal.

With the way Leora flinched, April knew it wasn't good.

"I'm the dog groomer?"

"You're the what?" He smiled at her, and the lopsided slope of his face made April shudder inside.

She turned slightly and pointed her thumb back at the little red and white van behind her. "I'm the dog groomer?"

He laughed. "Aren't you sure?"

April stared at him, confused. "Yes. I am."

"Well, I'm sure Leora here told you that no one is getting work done today, not even that fucking mutt."

"I was just going to go." April wanted to run to the van and try to get away but she saw the barrel of the gun against the side of Leora's head and she didn't like the look on the man's face.

"Instead of that, I think you should come in and visit with us."

What could she say to that?

"Uh, sure."

April crossed the threshold and the man with the gun moved with Leora, keeping himself to her side, he moved, but he kept his eyes on her.

"Keep coming." He smiled at her. "Keep coming. There." He lifted his chin toward the door and the movement dropped his chin-length hair back toward his ears enough for her to see the scar that cut across his cheek into his hairline. "Lock the door behind us. Come on."

"Lock the door. Okay."

She blew out a breath and locked the door. Turning around, she looked at the man again.

He turned his head toward the doorway at the other end of the room. "Go on. Walk through there."

April nodded and started to move, but she didn't realize how fast she was going until he barked out a laugh. "Slow down, sweetie."

Her stomach fell or rose, she couldn't tell. She just knew that she felt sick to her stomach.

"Slow down." She repeated the words to herself as she walked.

"That's a good pace right there. Keep going."

Keep going.

All she wanted to do was run.

But run where?

Her van was outside.

She'd locked the door behind her.

And her hands were shaking.

She could feel it at the ends of her arms. Shaking.

Rubbing her palms against the soft denim of her overalls, she walked through the doorway and stopped short. The living room. She'd seen it once when Mrs. Helm had interviewed her, asking her to bring a portfolio of the dogs that she'd groomed.

She'd seen it that once and felt scared about sitting down on their fancy chairs.

Now the room looked like a tornado had gone through. Marble topped end tables were toppled on their sides. A chair was on its back and a man who looked somewhat like the large portrait above the fireplace of the Helms when they were first married, was sitting on the couch, his arms secured behind him and his face looked like he'd been hit a whole bunch of times.

"Mister Helm?"

He looked up at her, one eye almost swollen shut. "Who the fuck are you?"

Feeling more stupid than ever, she gave him a wincing smile. "I'm the dog groomer."

He shook his head. "Oh, this is just getting better and better."

April was shoved from behind and she stumbled forward, grabbing the edge of the coffee table, which was still on its feet.

"Stay out of the way, girl, and maybe we'll forget you're here."

She didn't want to say a word, but everything he said was so snarky that she knew he was just a miserable person.

She made her way to the side of the couch and that's when she saw Princess.

The snow white husky was laying on his side, a growing blood pool turning some of his fur a scarlet red. "Oh, Princess!"

She moved to the dog and got down on her knees beside it. "What happened?"

Someone crouched down beside her and she couldn't tell who it was. Didn't care, really. She was trying to see how Princess had been injured.

"Don't worry, sweetie."

Oh, it was him.

"It wasn't our fault, really."

"It wasn't?" She looked up and saw the knife in his pocket. "Was it a knife? Or a... a bullet?"

"I don't usually answer questions," he explained, "but I think you really care about this devil dog."

"Princess is okay once you get to know him."

"Him?" The man laughed out loud and Princess whimpered on the floor. "Leave it to Fred to name a fucking boy dog 'Princess.'"

"It was my wife," Fred's voice was tight, pointed.

Leora was crying softly on the chair on the other side of her husband.

"Can I... May I have a cloth to bind the wound?"

April felt the man's eyes on her, but she didn't meet his gaze. She was still trying to find the wound on Princess' side.

A slight shift of her fingers made the dog whimper and what felt like a gush of fresh blood fell into her palm.

April lifted her gaze and found the man still watching her carefully. "Please? Something to wrap around Princess so I can stop the bleeding?"

He stared at her with a curious light in his eyes, but didn't move or speak to help her.

Pulling her hand out from under the beautiful dog, April ignored the angry gasps and the shout of caution from the men in the room.

Unhooking one shoulder strap of her overalls, she let go of Princess' side and pulled her t-shirt off. She heard the laughter of the men with guns and didn't care. She had on a sports bra under her shirt, but even if she didn't. She had to do something to try and save Princess.

When she had the shirt off, she twisted it around and managed to wrap it around the dog.

She heard the man laughing and made the mistake of looking up.

"You really are too sweet for words, aren't you?"

"I just don't see reason for stabbing a dog. Princess is high-strung but sweet."

He shook his head. "That dog came at me like it was rabid. I gave it a chance. Teeth against my knife." He grinned. "The dog lost."

She looked back down at the dog and heard a hollow click.

Leora gasped and Fred cursed under his breath.

"Come on, Fred. Have you made a decision? Your money, or your life?"

She refused to look up. Poor Princess had already been senselessly injured and she wasn't stupid.

She was going to be just another victim here.

If Mr. Helm thought that he'd live through this, he was crazy. These men were armed to the teeth like they were in some kind of late night TV show. The Closer, Chicago PD, or Criminal Minds.

She didn't have anyone like Derek Morgan or Jay Halstead ready to break in and save her life, but maybe she could keep Princess alive long enough for help to get to the scene.

But her own life? She wasn't stupid.

If she'd left when Leora had tried to get her to go. That might have made a difference, but she'd stuck around trying to help.

Foolish?

Sure.

But how was she to know?

CRACK

April jumped at the sound and Leora's painful howl.

Before Fred could get to her, the man standing closer to her pointed the barrel of his gun in Fred's face.

"Don't tempt me, Fred. Right now I'm going to let you type in the codes with your own fingers. So I'm taking the wife's."

April peeked around the edge of the sofa arm and saw Leora clutching one hand over the other against her chest. April could see blood slipping between her fingers and down her forearm.

She couldn't imagine the kind of pain the woman was going through.

Turning away from the horrifying scene, she looked out the window and almost gasped in shock.

There were men outside, but she didn't think they were with the men in the house already.

She lowered her gaze to Princess' flank and watched it rise and fall.

April gently stroked Princess' ear and whispered softly to her. Nonsense words and sounds that she thought might comfort the poor thing.

She knew that she might die at any minute, but she couldn't just sit there waiting. She had to do something productive and if it was taking care of this sweet and sometimes manic dog, then that's what she'd do.

"Come on, Fred. You want me to take another finger or two from your wife?"

Leora hollered at the threat.

Fred swore bitterly at the man. "I can't give it to you. If they know something happened to me, they'll automatically change the codes. This is exactly why they do it. So people like you can't threaten us to get what you want."

"Well, you don't have the computer guys that I have. We

can lock up the system as long as we need to, to get what I want. And I want your fuckin' money." He paused for a moment. "So give me the code."

"You can't use it. Let us go."

"Give him the fucking code, Freddy!"

Leora was screaming and stamping her feet.

April looked out the window out of the corner of her eye. The men outside were still coming, but it felt like they were crawling.

*Faster!*

She wanted to scream and tell them to get there faster!

"Give him the damn thing!"

A rush of sound and light caught April's eye and she looked up.

Leora was struggling, but with her husband. Her hands around his throat. The sight was gory and repulsive, but as the men rushed forward to pull husband and wife apart, April reached for the latch on the sliding door, thinking that whoever was outside was trying to save them.

The glass panel beside her hand disintegrated into what seemed like thousands of shards of glass.

April threw herself over Princess, shielding the dog with her body as more shots rang out. Some from the right where the armed men were and some from the left from outside the window.

The devastating explosions of sound seemed to go on and on and on.

And then suddenly, they stopped.

# CHAPTER TWO

She wasn't exactly sure when the gunshots stopped.

They were still ringing in her ears when she felt the rush of air conditioning from a dashboard.

"Miss? Miss? Are you okay?"

April felt a hand touch her leg and she shoved it off. "Don- don't touch me."

She wrapped her arms around herself and opened her arms again just as quickly. "Blood. I have blood on me."

"Probably from the dog, Miss."

"... the dog..."

Princess.

White fur.

Red blood.

"... oh my g- Stop the car!"

Her stomach was rioting in her belly, April stopped short of covering her mouth with her hands when she saw the flash of red on her skin.

Instead of emptying her stomach all over the pristine grey interior of the car, April held it down.

Barely.

"Thanks."

April turned her head and looked at the man in the driver's seat.

He looked like he worked for the government.

Dark suit.

Staid tie.

Simple hairstyle that didn't stand a chance of falling into his eyes.

"Who are you?"

He let out a breath. "Federal Marshal Dan Hamilton."

He said the words as if it would mean something to her.

When she didn't say much in return, he continued.

"You didn't look like you heard me the first time."

The first time?

"It was a joint action with another federal office. We had intel about a possible kidnapping and theft.

"With this particular group, we expected them to hold the husband and wife to demand information, but we weren't expecting you to drive up in that little car of yours."

She nodded her head, but the motion only stirred up her stomach. She wanted to ask where her van was, but she just couldn't seem to really care nor could she manage to speak.

Would she ever see her little van the same way again? Would she feel the pride in it? Or would she see it and remember the blood?

"You're the only live witness we've ever recovered."

He leaned forward and looked out the window on her side of the car.

"We intend to keep you that way."

April stared at the dashboard studiously.

The last thing she wanted to see was the... was her hands.

The color red-

Bile climbed up onto the back of her tongue.

It nearly took every bit of strength to hold it all down.

"It's probably merciful that you were 'out' when we extracted you from the house. You didn't have to see the carnage they left behind."

Her eyebrows rose at his words. She couldn't form a question.

She could barely feel anything at all.

"That's the reason why I put you in my car. I'm taking you somewhere safe. I have to go back to the office and then we'll get these guys.

"But until then, you're going to be protected by the best Federal Marshal I've ever known."

Oh?

April dragged in a breath and finally let out a hint of the tension that she'd been carrying.

## - BIG 'N BURLY DUO 3 -

Amos Kane was a man who needed his solitude.

His human solitude.

Standing on his porch, watching the first rays of dawn clawing themselves through the treetop, he waited almost patiently for his dog to finish his business in the snow.

And then even after his big, hulking mastiff finished marking his favorite copse of trees, he moved around, nose in the snow, lumbering gait moving him through one drift of snow after another.

"Come on, boy!"

Tank didn't even lift his nose up from the powdery snow, almost using it as a plow as he moved.

"Tank! Come on!"

Amos had almost lost sight of the mountain of fur when

Tank's large tail that looked more like a lamb's wool duster than a dog's tail, swished through the air.

If the woods around them had been still and devoid of any wind, his thick tail might make a sound like a helicopter, whumping back and forth.

But Amos didn't have the time to let the big bulldozer of a dog prowl to his heart's content.

He had a cup of coffee waiting for him in the kitchen and he'd left his jacket draped over the back of a chair at the kitchen table.

Grumbling to himself, Amos folded his arms across his chest. "Next time when you're whining and pawing at the door, I'm gonna make you wait until I'm good and warm first."

Amos rolled his eyes heavenward and sighed.

He might say that.

Hell, he might even say it to Tank, but he'd never actually make the dog wait.

Amos licked at his lips, feeling the rough texture under his tongue, and then whistled.

The piercing sound was eventually answered by the giant mastiff's head.

Looking more like a scruffy lion than a massive dog, Tank's thick coat was more of a mane around his head than anything else.

With a belly-aching groan, Amos dreaded the next time he was going to have to wrestle Tank to the ground and work the comb through his fur.

That was going to be an all-day event and likely end up in some hard feelings.

On *both* sides.

"Tank!" He whistled again and got more of a reaction from birds in the trees than his dog. "Get in here! Or I'm going in and getting something to eat without you."

That got Tank's attention.

The dog didn't speak a lick of English, but he knew all the pertinent words.

Walk.

Belly.

Grub.

Eat.

Bath.

Comb.

The last two usually resulted in Tank taking off like a shot and coming back home with twigs and leaves embedded in his coat and a goofy grin on his face.

Before Amos got to the front door, his toes tingling from the cold, Tank was dashing, in his own way, up the steps, his massive frame making the steps groan.

The snow under and in his paws mixed with the sanded and treated wood of the porch, sent Tank into a skid.

Amos managed to get the door open before the big mass of fur lumbered into the tiny cabin.

"Hey!" Amos let the door close behind him and reached for one of the thick cloths he kept by the door. "Get back here."

Tank stopped between Amos and his empty bowl, turning a baleful stare at Amos.

"Yeah. I know. It's empty." He held up the thick drying cloth. "Come here and let me get the snow off of your paws."

Now, Amos had never had a child of his own, nor had he spent any real time around children, but he swore that the suffering stare that Tank gave him would have come with tiny stomping feet and a pouting bottom lip if Tank had been human.

The fact that he was a dog didn't change much.

Amos knew that he was likely spoiling the dog, but who was going to complain?

Well, Tank did when he didn't get his way, but that didn't happen often.

As Amos held out the cloth in both hands, waiting, Tank lifted one paw with a loud huff and plopped it down onto the cloth.

Yeah.

His dog was spoiled.

"You don't mind that you're spoiled, right?"

Tank tilted his head, looking back at him.

"Right. No complaints from you."

Amos went back to drying off Tank's massive paws and was almost ready to nudge the massive boy over onto his side and prepare to do battle for the back set, when he heard a noise outside.

Amos clambered onto his feet to make his way to the door and was almost knocked to the ground by the massive shoulder of his pup.

"Stay here. Your paws are wet."

He made it to the door with Tank still hunkered down on the rug.

Improvement.

Not bad.

And then he saw the vehicle pushing through the snow on the driveway.

It was large, black, and institutional.

"Fuck."

"WOOF!"

"Exactly."

Reaching the table, he pulled his jacket from the back of the chair and managed to shrug it on while he stuffed his stockinged feet into his boots.

If he was going out to tell them to go to hell, he would at least be warm.

Ish.

Then again, he reasoned, his indignation would help too.

He added the final accoutrement to his outfit, grabbing up his shotgun from its place beside his door. Tucking it into a modified pocket carry to secure it, he crossed the porch and down the steps to the drive.

The man behind the wheel wasn't necessarily unwelcome. It just depended on what he was there for.

Just before the SUV came to a halt parallel to his steps, Amos took a quick survey of the land around him.

The door cracked open and Dan gave him a guarded smile while he kept his hands slightly raised and away from his body. "I'm going to be grateful that you don't have that pointed at my head."

"Sure. That's one way to look at it."

Dan's brows lifted just a bit. "I thought we left things on a positive note."

"I told you I'm not going back. You showing up here makes me think that you don't listen all that well. I'm not going back, Dan."

"I'm not asking you to." His old friend dropped his chin down toward his chest. "I need your help."

"You need to-"

"We went after the Hale Family."

Amos shook his head. "The Hale Family?"

"Well," Dan shrugged, "that's who we think are behind these kidnappings. They've been trying to rebuild their cash reserves and prove that they're willing to go to the next level to put themselves back on the map."

Amos nodded. He'd wanted to go after the Hale crime

family for several years, but he'd never been given the okay to do so.

"That's good. A few years too late, but good. Still, I don't see how I can help. Like I told you before-"

"I have a witness."

Well that was news.

"I need you to keep them safe."

Oh no.

Amos' hand flexed on the grip of his shotgun. "No. You can turn right around-"

"I have to head back into the office so we can go after the Hales."

"So, take your witness to the office. The FBI has safe houses all over the city."

"I'm putting the witness into WITSEC, Amos."

"Then do it, but this isn't a damn safe house. I retired, Dan and you fucking know it. You're not going to drag me back into this!"

Dan pushed his door open, almost pushing Amos back.

"Don't be a fucking asshole, Amos. This isn't the time. This isn't about you."

"He isn't going to let me stay. Can we please go?"

"Wait." Amos grabbed the edge of the door and held tight. "What's going on?"

What had looked like a pile of discarded rags on the passenger seat of the SUV sat up and Dan peeled back some of the layers to reveal a woman. Well, *the woman* he'd heard just a moment before.

And holy hell, she was barely dressed!

Amos reached his hand in and took a hold of Dan's lapel. "What the fuck, man? You've got a damn coat on and she's half-dressed!"

He saw the way Dan avoided his gaze and he wanted to

plant his fist in the man's face, but that would have to wait.

"Damn it."

Amos walked around the front of the SUV and came up to the passenger side door, but drew in a breath and let it out before reaching for the handle.

When he pulled it open, he wasn't prepared for the feelings that assaulted him when she met his hard gaze.

Shit. He wanted to do more than hold the door for her, he wanted to pull her into his arms and carry her inside his cabin.

He must have hit his head on something.

Or caught a case of cabin fever to feel like that.

Amos didn't want to touch her because he wasn't sure that he could be gentle.

There were too many emotions running through him to be sure that he could keep his shit together.

There was a damn good reason why he kept to himself out in the middle of nowhere.

He just wasn't fit to be around good people.

Of that, he was sure.

So instead of reaching for her, he did the safer thing. He set his shotgun down against the side of the car and tugged his jacket off.

The chill of the mountain air didn't touch him.

He was too thick skinned for that, physically and emotionally.

It took a moment to get his jacket off, but it felt like forever.

"Here," he grumped at her. "Put this on."

The layers of fabric fell even further away from her and he saw Dan continue to peel it back.

Amos barely resisted barking at the man like a guard dog to tell him to take his hands off of her, but that wasn't going to help.

The woman reached for the jacket, but her hands were shaking like crazy.

She saw the way his eyes fixed on her hands and she bit into her bottom lip.

He didn't know if she was afraid or ashamed, but either way, he didn't like it.

Not one fucking bit.

"Here, let me help you."

It was the means to an end, he told himself.

The longer that they were out in the cold, the more angry he'd get.

He'd managed to keep his hands mostly to himself where it came to Dan, but the more this woman shook and shivered, the more angry he became.

She reached out to him, took hold of his forearm so that she could slide off of her seat and onto the runner of the SUV and Amos had to grit his teeth.

It was static electricity.

It had to be.

Why else would he feel like lightning had lanced its way straight into his cold, dead heart and start it beating again?

He didn't bother with putting her arms through the sleeves.

He wrapped his coat around her body and tucked her against his chest. With a quick nudge of his foot against the stock of the shotgun, he picked that up with his free hand.

He marched right up the stairs and onto his porch.

Dan earned himself a few points by opening the door, but even inside, Amos didn't want to put her down.

Yeah.

He wasn't just in trouble.

He was well and truly fucked.

# CHAPTER THREE

April wanted to argue. No, not argue. She wanted to tell this... this mountain of a man that she could walk on her own.

She wanted to.

But she couldn't deny that the way he held her, wrapped up in his coat, made her feel warm.

Made her feel safe.

It had to be a moment of fantasy.

A dream.

She just couldn't trust how she was feeling.

Less than a day ago, she was going to another grooming appointment and now she was shivering and lost in her head.

And heaven help her. She didn't want him to let her go.

In his arms, she was warm and comforted.

When he sat her down on the couch in front of a roaring fire, she wanted to reach out and grab a hold of his flannel and hold him there with her.

Remember, she told herself, you can walk on your own two feet.

He grumbled something under his breath and stepped

back from her.

There was something in his expression. Something in his eyes that made her feel unsettled. No, it made her feel secure. Under his watchful eye, she also felt... alone.

Taking hold of the edges of his coat, she pulled it tighter around her, leaning into its warmth.

Strange.

She hadn't even formerly met the man and she felt such comfort wrapped up in his clothes.

Tilting her chin down, she inhaled his scent.

In and out, she breathed it in.

Breathed him in.

And those breaths, that scent, calmed her nerves and she relaxed into the deep cushioned perfection of his sofa.

There was a rumble of sound and soft footsteps headed toward the door.

She knew she wasn't going to be left alone and kept her focus on the comforting sounds and scents around her.

The smoky crackle of logs in the fireplace.

The dancing heat across the one cheek that she left exposed to the room.

The woodsy scent of his jacket, including the woolen comfort of the jacket's lining.

It was all... perfection.

Huff Huff Huff...

She turned her head to the side and saw the largest dog she'd ever seen in her life looking right back at her.

His breaths panted out as if the heat of the room didn't sit well with him, but there he was just outside the reach of her arm.

April wanted to wiggle her fingers through his thick mat of fur, but she didn't want to feel any cold remaining in the air.

She didn't like feeling so... fearful.

April turned her face, so no one had to see how much fear she felt displayed across her features. She didn't want to see it. Why should she subject anyone else to the sight?

Huff Woof Huff...

Oh...

A big heavy head leaned into her temple and she rocked along with the push. Rocked and felt the warmth of the massive dog heating half of her body.

Snuffling into her ear, the dog was almost on top of her, tumbling her to the side.

When the sofa cushioned her head she laughed and felt the scratch of the dog's tongue on her cheek.

"Whoa there..."

April snorted a giggle as the dog licked her cheek again. She put out her hands to grasp the thick mane of fur around the dog's head and neck, but as big as the dog was, he moved his head quickly and kept out of her grasp.

"Goodness." She had to squeeze her eyes shut to avoid the wet slurp. "You're huge!"

She felt the dog move further toward her head and she had a feeling that if the dog sat down or even crouched down on his haunches, she would be smushed into the sofa cushion like a marshmallow on a graham cracker.

The heat from the coat wrapped around her was now coupled with the massive canine heater standing over her.

"I hope the legs on this sofa aren't going to snap with both of us on here."

The dog didn't try to reassure her.

He didn't even seem to consider the question.

All he did was step carefully over her and fill in the gap between the sofa and the coffee table.

She had a feeling that he was lying down in the narrow

space and somehow he was big enough to put his massive head on the cushion beside her head.

"Well, hello."

Big dark eyes stared back at her and a cold wet nose touched against her own dry and warm one.

"Aren't you a handsome boy?" She yawned and cuddled into the coat. "I'm going to..."

He leaned in closer, whining softly as he pushed his nose under her hand.

April felt a strange reassurance, feeling the thick fur under her hand. And the warm breath of a massive dog across her cheek.

It was just too surreal to understand.

Just like the last twenty-four hours. From her carefully crafted life to lying exhausted on a stranger's sofa, just a breath or two from sleep.

She heard the soft, almost plaintive whine from the dog and moved her hand until she had circled as much of the dog's massive neck as she could.

And slipped away.

## – BIG 'N BURLY DUO 3 –

Amos wanted to let the door slam shut behind him, but he couldn't.

The woman he'd just left alone in his cabin, his refuge, was clearly shivering and exhausted.

He might need to take his frustration out on Dan, but not her.

And Dan was damn lucky that he didn't shove Dan down the porch steps and into the snow.

"Who is she?"

Dan opened his mouth to speak, but Amos wasn't having any of his shit.

He knew the other man well enough to see the flintlike spark in Dan's gaze.

"Name, asshole." He shook his head when Dan fucking smiled. "Don't give me any of your stupid jokes. You caught me at the wrong moment."

Amos should have known that Dan wasn't going to let the stupid act drop.

He probably thought they were still friends.

And Dan proved it a moment later. "You want me to bring her back later? A few hours? You need time to piss and moan before you can do the right thing?"

Amos had his hands full of Dan's dry cleaned dress shirt.

"You don't fucking get to talk about the right thing! You don't get to go anywhere near that kind of argument. That's a line you and the whole fucking Marshal Service crossed a few years ago.

"There's no coming back from that."

"For you?" Dan leaned in, putting emphasis on his words and narrowing his gaze at the same time. "You planning on being angry for the rest of your life?"

"No."

Amos saw that his answer had shaken Dan. It wasn't worry he saw in the other man's eyes, but confusion.

"No?" Dan pressed. "Then what?"

Amos felt bile coat the surface of his tongue. "Maybe yours. Certainly the men that killed my friend."

"I get it." Dan shook his head. "I get it, man. It's easier to keep blaming everyone else. No worries then. You don't have to look at the truth."

"And what," Amos almost snarled at the other man, "is that?"

"The truth that we give bad guys a second chance to get the big bads." He pushed on before Amos could interject. "And yeah, sometimes we get it wrong. That doesn't mean that we stop doing it. It doesn't mean that we get to question the reasoning behind it.

"You and I? You and-" He paused when Amos' glare nearly boiled over. "We're cogs in the machine, man. We're given orders and we follow it. We," one corner of his mouth tipped up in the ghost of a grin, "don't get to question the guys that make the big bucks. And believe me, you don't want their job.

"If you feel this bad, imagine if it was you sending people into the crossfire? You couldn't do what they do. You wouldn't want to pull that trigger."

He was right, but probably not for the reasons Dan attributed to his decision.

Amos believed that there might be a way to save this woman. Her body. Her soul.

He knew that his body had seen better fucking days.

And Amos had a feeling that he didn't have a soul left to save.

This, he reasoned, this is why he'd walked away and found himself a place out in the woods where there wasn't a damn bit of humanity anywhere around him.

He couldn't save someone if he wasn't able to save himself.

"Come on, man. I need you help on this."

Amos didn't fucking believe him.

"There's a list of safe houses as long as my forearm. Take her there. Get her a guard."

Even as he spit the words out, he knew he wasn't going to drag her back out into the cold.

He certainly didn't want to trust her to Dan's less-than-capable care.

No matter how much he wanted her to leave, Dan was partially right.

Amos couldn't let her leave with Dan.

While he might find a place to put her up for a little bit of time, he couldn't guarantee her safety.

*Neither can I*, he reminded himself.

It was true.

Still, he'd been out of the game long enough that he doubted anyone would consider him as a viable shelter for a witness.

And anyone and their uncle, in more than a dozen foreign governments, knew that he'd left the Marshal Service just like some military generals practiced warfare: scorched earth.

They'd likely consider dead people before they would look at him as a viable candidate.

Sighing, Amos felt his jaw start to ache from the way he clenched his jaw together.

"What. Is. Her. Name."

Dan shrank a little in stature and Amos remembered that look. He'd seen it in the mirror a time or two when the job weighed heavily on his shoulders.

"April. April Reynolds."

"What was she doing there?"

A little bit of a smile made Amos narrow his eyes at the other man.

"She's a dog groomer. She brought her van with her. Something that looks more like a toy than an actual business car."

Amos reached a hand up and settled the woolen beanie he liked to wear. "What kind of a toy?"

Dan shrugged. "One of those VW van kits. Red and white. A puppy logo painted on the side. When it turned up in the driveway, we didn't know why it was there. It didn't match any known vehicle for the gang. And as undercover vans go, it was way too visible to be government issued."

Shrugging, Amos had to agree. "Government employees lack the creativity."

Dan's upper lip tugged up at one end. "You hate us that much?"

At first, Amos wasn't sure he had an answer.

Then he didn't know if he wanted to answer.

What the hell.

"I hate the decisions that are made over our heads when we're the ones who have to follow through. We're the ones who get our hands dirty. We're the ones putting our lives on the line.

"And we're the ones who are left standing over the dead bodies of the ones we lose."

He saw the way Dan's gaze turned toward the tree line and he placed his fisted hands on his hips.

"You want me to take her somewhere else? If you can't do this, Amos, just fucking say so. We've been driving for hours and if you can't hide her here, I've got to get back on the road."

Amos knew he was right. As far as safe houses went, unless they'd added new ones since he'd left the Marshal's office, the next one was hours away.

He'd seen the look on her face when he'd taken her inside and felt the way she shook from exhaustion.

Regardless of the shit he'd dealt with, the woman inside his cabin was the very definition of an innocent.

Amos shook his head, more at the situation than anything else.

He was a surly asshole. He never made any bones about that. He'd left his work telling them hell would freeze over before he'd have anything to do with the Marshal Service or WITSEC ever again.

He turned in a slow circle, staring at what had been his refuge until Dan drove his SUV up the drive.

As angry as he was, Amos couldn't let that anger boil over onto the woman in his cabin.

She hadn't asked to be brought to the cabin.

She didn't even know about him or the shit he'd been through. Taking it out on her went against the man he'd tried to save when he quit the service.

He knew what he had to do.

He turned back and saw Dan waiting for his decision.

"I'll keep her here until you get things settled so she can go home safely. You said there's a group going after the men right now?"

"Yeah. Right now." Dan stepped forward with his hand out to shake, but Amos kept his arms where they were. "It shouldn't be more than a day, two at the most, that's why I'm trying to get back. I want to be there when they bust these men.

"Two escaped from the home. Once we have them in custody, we'll have April come in and identify them. After that, she'll be able to move into an official WITSEC placement.

"Right now, things are just up in the air, I-"
"Fine."

Dan drew back a little, tilting his chin down and narrowing his eyes. "Yeah?"

Amos hated how excited the other man sounded. There was nothing exciting about this fucked up situation.

"I'll watch out for her."

Dan nodded. "That's amazing. That's just-"

Amos turned away and walked up the steps to his porch and closed the door, shutting out the world behind him.

# CHAPTER FOUR

What the fuck was he going to do?

He walked into his house to talk to his guest and get a few things worked out, but she was asleep.

Passed out.

Sprawled on his couch.

Shaking his head, he leaned back against the wall beside the door and let out the breath that he'd been holding. That's when he noticed the big hulking shadow sat between the couch and the coffee table.

"Tank."

The Tibetan Mastiff opened one dark eye and looked in his direction.

"Let's go outside. Let her sleep."

Tank closed his eye and sat there, his massive head tucked under her chin.

"Tank." Amos lifted a brow at the dog, staring into his head.

The dog's eyelid twitched, but that was it.

Amos rolled his eyes and pulled his jaw apart as he hissed his dog's name. "Tank."

The dog breathed out and some of the wispy curls that had crept onto her cheeks lifted and dropped back down.

Balling his hands into fists, he pushed himself away from the wall and moved across the floor of the cabin on the opposite side of the open fireplace and stopped in front of the storage closet.

Amos listened but didn't hear Tank's familiar plodding steps following after him.

"Traitor." He let out a sigh and opened the closet door. There was a narrow shelf pantry in front of him and reaching into back of a low profile of spice bottles, he flipped a switch.

A soft click echoed in the seemingly narrow pantry and the shelves swung inward and flattened against the wall.

The suddenly empty doorway revealed the cool gunmetal gray surface of his gun safe. Without a situation pressing on his time, Amos opened the safe with a combination.

He could have used his thumbprint if he wanted to, but it helped to keep his practice with the dial.

It paid to practice.

Muscle memory saved lives.

He may have retired from serving the government and his country, but he knew the dangers that existed outside his door. If they came knocking, he would always be ready.

With a good tug, he opened the door to the safe and did a quick inventory of its contents.

There wasn't a chance that any of his collection were missing from the safe. That wasn't why he opened the storage area to check.

He wasn't alone anymore.

Of course, Amos always counted Tank in his life. The dog

kept him from going stir crazy, but try as he might, Tank didn't talk back when he talked to him.

His dog had a wealth of reactions when he felt like showing his feelings, but speech wasn't big on Tank's priorities.

Ball? Sure.

Slobbering on the windows? Absolutely.

Those were some of his favorite things.

As irritating as Dan could be, he wasn't an alarmist. The blood on April's clothes only began to tell the tale of what she'd gone through.

When he knew that she'd spend some time asleep, he'd go through his entire collection. Clean them and make sure they were all in perfect working order.

He knew the process well enough that it could be a rote activity for him. Amos could do it in his sleep, but he always put care into the job.

He'd seen too many misfires and even seen a weapon explode in the hands of a range officer.

You could never prevent every problem, but he could and would be prepared.

With one last look, he grabbed the edge of the heavy door and closed it.

As soon as he removed his arm from the storage area, he gave the pantry shelf a soft tug and felt it swing back into place.

Amos walked back into the main room and moved to the sink to wash his hands. The warm water gave him some relief from the cold and he reached for a clean towel to dry off with.

The light outside was bright enough, but he gave the clock on the wall a quick glance. Out in the woods, it made sense to check a clock as cloud cover and weather could conceal the accurate time if he tried to track it by the light.

That left him wondering about food. He doubted that Dan had stopped to get his witness something to eat. It was doubtful that he'd take a chance having her in the car, splattered in blood, and go to a drive through.

He'd never leave her in the car and run in either.

That would be Bullshit 101 for a WITSEC Marshal.

Amos didn't expect that from Dan. He might be part of this fuck up, but he wasn't stupid.

The corner of his mouth tilted up in a smile.

He'd brought her to the cabin.

Maybe Dan was smarter than Amos had given him credit for.

Amos shook his head and turned when he heard Tank's dog tag jingle behind him.

She was awake.

And standing beside her was Tank.

Amos didn't say a word, but his head was filled with them. She looked frail, world worn, and though he hated to say it, he was somewhat envious of the way she had a grip on Tank's collar.

"'m sorry," she swallowed after whispering out the words. "I fell asleep."

"You need it. More, probably."

She lifted her free hand and touched her face, shielding part of her face from his eyes. "I look like I've been through hell."

He couldn't argue with that.

"I don't have anything with me." Her lips pressed together and rolled back and forth before she pried them apart. "Do you... Could I wash my face?"

Amos felt his brow furrow and a pain settle behind his eyes.

He was a total shithead sometimes.

"Ye- I mean no."

He saw her hand tighten around Tank's collar.

"I mean, you can do more than wash your face." He pointed a thumb over his shoulder. "I have a tub you can use. Plenty of hot water."

Her smile was as surprising as his reaction to it.

He smiled in return.

And Tank? Well, Tank canted his head to the side and stared up at Amos as if he couldn't believe it either.

"You... ah, you need help walking?"

Her smiled softened and her gaze dropped to the massive dog beside her.

Amos watched as she moved her hand through Tank's thick fur coat.

"Tank seems willing to help me. Right, boy?"

The massive head swung up to look at her and from where Amos stood, he could see the look of adoration in Tank's whole face.

It seemed like he was the only one fighting what he'd already declared was an intrusion.

Tank didn't think so, or he wouldn't have watched over her while she slept. He wouldn't stand there beside her and let her lean against him.

"I'll," Amos swept his tongue over his bottom lip and took a step back toward the bedroom, "I'll get the water started."

He turned his back and moved, his feet plodding across the hardwood floor. "It's a tub and shower. You can use it however you want."

The back of the house was colder by a few degrees than the front room. He felt it on his face and then the backs of his hands as he moved out of the hallway into the bathroom.

He ignored his reflection in the mirror and bent over the

edge of the tub to reach the hot water knob. He turned it with a twist of his wrist that was almost too firm.

Too hard.

He didn't like this.

He didn't like the feelings he was struggling with.

It wasn't all that hard. Right?

Sharing his space with her wasn't going to be for long.

Dan had all but promised it wouldn't last more than a couple of days.

He could hold on to that.

Amos moved the back of his hand under the faucet and pulled back from the heat.

He had a damn good heater and he probably should have paid more attention to the steam rising from the bottom of the tub.

Leaning in again, Amos twisted the cold water knob and heard the bump of the pipes as the water rushed out even faster from the faucet.

He kept his gaze on the rising surface of the water creeping up the side of the tub until he heard the soft click of Tank's nails on the floor.

"You don't have to fill the tub," her voice was stronger by a bit. "It would be a waste. I just need to scrub... to scrub this off my skin and put something on that's clean. Which means-"

"I've got things that you can wear." Amos stood and turned, almost knocking her off of her feet. "Hey." He reached out and took hold of her shoulders to steady her. "Sorry about that."

Her cheeks flushed in the narrow enclosure of his bathroom and he felt the heat of the steam glancing across his skin.

"I guess it's a tight fit."

He heard the lilt of humor in her voice and nodded almost imperceptibly.

"I guess they really mean it when they say 'three's a crowd.'"

"What they meant," he leaned over and gave Tank a good scratch behind the ears, "was that a dog almost bigger than the doorway, or big enough to take up most of the floor should remember their manners."

Amos slowed his hand and drew the tips of his fingers down the dog's nose and made a soft snap with his fingertips.

"Tank. Out."

His dog turned a baleful look in her direction.

Amos ground his back teeth together, trying to hold back the instinctual grumble about to push up through his throat.

He opened his mouth to remind Tank just who the alpha dog was and then he stopped.

April leaned over Tank's broad back and hugged him with a soft head to toe shake.

Tank's face said he enjoyed the embrace, but he stepped back, wiggling his backside.

"Careful. He's heavy enough to knock you down."

"Just because he can, doesn't mean he will."

Her voice was so soft, he wasn't sure he was hearing her correctly.

She watched as Tank backed up like an eighteen-wheeler and then sat down just outside the bathroom door. "He's really special."

Amos agreed with her inside, but he had become more than a little sour in his time away from others, so it made it a little difficult to just agree with her estimation on the surface.

"He can be a big ol' pain in my ass."

If what he said bothered her, she didn't say a word.

He watched her gravitate to the tub and he held out his hand, moving past her own.

She drew back just a hint and he continued on until his

fingers dipped into the water in the tub. He left them in there for a few seconds and then lifted his hand.

Putting his hand over hers, he let a few drops of water fall on the back of her hand. "That okay?"

When she didn't answer, he looked up at her.

She was looking down at her hand with a strange, confusion.

"What's wrong?"

She turned her head a little to the side and then her hand, almost as if she was mesmerized.

"April?"

She flinched and her eyes widened as she met his gaze. "What?"

He felt a pinch as his brow furrowed.

She gasped in a breath, swallowed, and then offered him a brittle smile. "Sorry. You said something?"

Amos saw her expression change again.

Stilled.

Softened.

And then her gaze dropped down.

He looked there, too.

He was holding her hand.

His thumb moving across the back, almost brushing over her knuckles.

He should stop.

He really should.

It had to be the heat.

The steam.

Calming.

Relaxing.

She shivered, and he felt it through her hand.

"Shit."

Amos let go and she took a step back and another until she

was leaning against the doorframe. He put his hand on the edge of the tub and turned both knobs down. "I'll, uh, leave this going. You stop it when you want to."

He walked through the door, carefully avoiding her and stepping over Tank's paw to get out of the room and across the hall into his bedroom.

It was like walking through a wall of cold. The air this far from the fire and out of the heat of the bathroom was like a quick slap to his face.

"Good," he told himself. "You needed that."

Grumbling to himself, he pulled open the top drawer of his dresser and stared. He had a shit-ton of flannel.

Shaking his head, he felt his shoulders shake with a laugh.

At himself.

"Holding her hand."

"Touching her like that?"

Amos closed his eyes and drew in a breath through his nose.

It felt good.

It felt really good.

He stood there, breathing in the dark.

For how long, he didn't know, but he finally felt a little centered.

Ever since he'd seen the armored Lincoln Navigator in his driveway, he'd been off balance. Tilting back and forth, struggling to keep himself focused.

He was finally getting it back.

He only had to do this for a couple of days.

A few at the most.

All he had to do was wait.

His eyes snapped open and his ears picked up a sound.

Tank.

Grabbing a shirt out of the dresser, he wheeled around and looked at Tank in the hall.

Tank was leaning against the closed door of the bathroom, pushing his shoulder against it, repeatedly pushing, whining... pushing.

"Shit."

# CHAPTER FIVE

Tank might have a never-ending stomach and the habit for shedding everywhere in the cabin, but he wasn't an alarmist.

He didn't bark at squirrels or growl when there wasn't an actual danger.

Having him push against the bathroom door and whine the way he was meant something.

And fuck, Amos felt that same alarm in his gut.

Shit.

Keeping a death grip on the shirt in his hand, he moved across the hall and used his own bulk to move the dog back.

Tank lifted his head and Amos saw the worry plainly written on the dog's face.

"Yeah. I know."

Raising his hand, Amos knocked on the door. "April?"

Nothing.

Amos leaned in and put his cheek and ear to the door. He knocked again with his free hand. "April?"

Nothing.

Except the heavy fall of water.

In his head, a flash of an image came to him.

April.

Drowned.

Amos gripped the doorknob and gave it a twist.

The solid metal doorknob stuck, but the door groaned under the weight of Amos' strength.

"April, stay back from the door!"

Unsure of where she was in the room, Amos knew he couldn't kick the door in. He might do more damage than good.

Tossing the plaid shirt over his shoulder, he put one hand on the knob and the other around the first. Drawing in a deep breath, he twisted the knob with all of his might, leaning his shoulder against the door.

Wood shifted against wood.

Metal creaked.

And then with a loud POP, the door pushed inward and Amos worked to stop it short.

Tank was at his back immediately, his head pushing against the back of Amos' thighs.

Reaching a hand back, Amos felt the dog's massive head under his palm. "There isn't room, bud. Let me go."

Tank continued to push on his hand and Amos swung his head around quickly to look at Tank.

"I'll take care of her, I promise."

Tank relaxed then. Sitting back on his haunches he nearly filled the hallway.

Amos gave the dog a nod and stepped inside.

A quick glance around the tiny room offered a moment of relief.

April was alive, but she was sitting in the tub, her head in her hands, shivering.

He moved to the tub and leaned over, putting his hand

under the spray. It was warm, not hot, but that only made the shivers more concerning.

"April? Are you hurt?"

He had to ask it a second time before her head snapped up and her gaze met his. She shook her head.

He could tell by the clear water that she wasn't actively bleeding, but hurt wasn't just physical.

He'd learned that from experience.

Too much of it.

"You cold?"

She shook her head again, but she shivered before him and her head ducked down as she wrapped her arms around her knees.

"Come here." He didn't know why he said it. It certainly hadn't been a conscious decision. "April, come here and let me get you warm."

He wasn't sure he could actually figure it out if she wasn't warming up under the heated spray of the shower, but letting her sit there and shake wasn't working for him, either.

Amos put the toilet seat down and set the flannel shirt down on top of it.

He got down on one knee so he could look at her in the eye and lifted her chin so he could see her face better.

She'd cleaned off any sign of blood on her skin and that gave him some semblance of relief. She hadn't deserved to be in the situation that she'd found herself in. He didn't want to make it any harder on her.

"Come on. Let's get you out of there and into something warm."

She took the hand that he offered her, but when she started to move, her feet slipped under the water.

He released her hand and reached for her waist. His

hands slipped along her slick skin and he ended up with a solid grip on her hips.

"Oh!" Her hands landed on his shoulders and her fingers managed to get some kind of purchase there, holding tight.

Amos sat down on the edge of the tub, bracing his booted feet apart on the floor. He made sure that her feet were on the warm mat so that she didn't have to step on the cool tiles.

Reaching out to the side, he picked up a thick bath towel and before he tried to put it in her hand, he felt her hands on his shoulders, still shaking.

He looked up and met her eyes.

She looked curiously at him, but he could also see the hint of pink in her cheeks.

She was naked and shivering. There was no way for him to ignore her bare skin and her curves, but while he might be a surly old asshole, he wasn't going to take advantage of her.

He needed to get her warm.

"Here, let me help."

He got up on his feet. He didn't move too quickly, afraid that he might startle her. When he was standing he realized, perhaps for the first time, that she was just a few inches shorter than he was. With just a little up tilt of her chin, she looked him right in the eye.

Wrapping the towel around her back, he started there, across her shoulder blades. The towel scrubbed lightly against her skin. She didn't move away or make any sounds that sounded like displeasure.

"I know your name," he told her, trying to speak about nothing and something at the same time. "I'm Amos. Amos Kane."

"Y-you worked with... with-"

"Sometimes. I didn't work with many people."

He worked his way down toward her lower back, keeping

her between the towel and his body, hoping that it might preserve some of the heat.

"You d-don't like people?"

"No." He smiled and leaned back a little to work the towel over her shoulders. "Not really. Then again, most people don't like me either."

He started down one arm, rubbing the towel against her skin.

"I guess it's why I went into the Marshal Service."

"M-marshal?" He reached her hand and rubbed it between both of his. "Like the Old W-west?"

"No." He didn't know why he almost laughed, his sense of humor, along with his social side had never been anywhere close to his strong suit. He knew he probably looked like a grizzly bear, and he didn't want to scare her. "Federal Marshals are the ones who protect witnesses and keep them safe. We relocate and watch over people who've been put in danger."

He started with her other hand and worked up toward her elbow.

The door had swung closed, keeping most of the heat inside the room, but April? She was still shivering.

He'd seen witnesses lose their lunch from stress.

He'd even seen them faint dead away.

Amos hoped that April wasn't about to get sick. There wasn't a doctor or a hospital anywhere near him. There were ways to get help, but none of them would keep her location safe.

He kept going, working the towel against her skin, hoping that wouldn't be necessary.

"So, you're like... Arnold Schwarzenegger in *Eraser*? You're going to give me a new name? Drop me off in a city where I don't know anyone?"

"I don't know about that," he explained and sat down on the closed toilet seat and moved the towel over her hips.

He wasn't as soft or gentle as he could have been but a little friction would warm her up more and it was already hard enough being this close to her bare skin. If he was gentle about it, he wasn't sure he could keep his mind on the job.

"I've never wrestled an alligator or landed in a junkyard with a messed up parachute."

"Well," he swore he heard her smiling, "maybe you could get me a job in a bar with drag shows. That seemed like a pretty cool place to work."

"Oh?" He leaned over and put his hand against the back of her thigh. Amos did his best to ignore the heat that seared through his body. He was more than aware of how close he was with his cheek mere inches from her belly. He heard her sudden indrawn breath as he lifted her leg to put it up on the seat lid between his thighs.

Before he could cheat and look toward the tops of her thighs, he started working the towel down her thigh.

*Talk to her*, he told himself. *Talk to her so you don't have to think about how close her foot is to-*

"So you have experience working in bars?"

"Well," her tone dropped a little, "I guess I wouldn't be put to work doing something I've done before."

"That is true." He shook his head.

She was right.

Then again, he wasn't thinking about that. He was trying not to think about the leg he had his hands around.

He heard the soft sound of her swallowing in the quiet of the room.

Amos didn't push. He kept his focus on what he was doing.

If he looked up to see what she was thinking, he'd have no

way to avoid looking at her belly and breasts. It didn't help that every inch of skin that he'd seen was perfect.

Soft.

Supple.

Sexy.

Apparently he'd been alone in his cabin too long.

He wasn't a monk, but he kind of lived like one. He didn't think about women. He had too much to do out in the woods. It took up most of his time and most days he fell into bed and slept like a fucking log.

Putting his hands on April had changed something inside of him.

That wall that he'd welded around his soul?

It had cracks, now.

Cracks that were widening by the moment.

"I think Dan said something about a van?"

"Pretty Puppy Mobile Dog Grooming." There was a new lightness in her voice. "I showed up to groom Princess, their dog. It was my fault, you know."

Amos' hands slowed to a stop on her calf.

Keeping his hands still, he looked up at her. "Were you a part of the crew that was holding them captive?"

She drew back, her face a picture of disbelief. "No. Of course not."

"Then it's not your fault."

He went back to work while she argued with the top of his head.

"I meant it's my fault that I got wrapped up in this. Missus Helm was trying to tell me to leave, but I didn't want to lose the appointment. It's not like I couldn't reschedule it later, but I'm just really getting my business on its feet."

"And she's a good client, I guess?"

He gently set her foot back on the floor and before he reached for her other leg, he heard her take in a deep breath.

And then exhale.

"She's a little odd, but I like her."

"Odd?"

He worked the towel around her thigh, trying desperately not to touch her skin. It was too much of a temptation.

Amos felt her shake, worried that she was still too cold. Worried until he heard her soft chuckles.

"Odd because she doesn't seem to know that her dog Princess is a boy. Still, after I saw how she dotes on Princess it didn't matter to me. I love grooming Princess even if he's a husky."

"What does that matter?" He shrugged. "I don't know much about dog breeds." He kept working down her leg.

"Huskies can be huge drama queens and Princess was no exception. If he can stand it, I put a band around his head and ears so he doesn't hear the blowing air when I dry him off. If he can't handle the band around his great big beautiful head, I get to hear the *song of his people* at the top of his lungs for what feels like forever."

Well, he learned something new to add to the laundry list of odd facts in his head.

"Maybe you can teach me a little about Tank. I don't even know much about him, besides the fact that he wasn't supposed to get that big."

She laughed.

A pure joyous sound.

That caught his attention. When he lifted his gaze to look at her, he tried to ignore the dark curls at the apex of her thighs.

Tried to.

He met her gaze even as he cursed himself for not keeping his eyes to himself.

Thankfully, April didn't seem to know that his eyes had strayed. She was smiling.

"What's so funny?" he asked her. "Me?"

She shook her head and he felt a few drops of water fall on his face. He'd forgotten to dry her hair.

He felt like a damn idiot.

April was standing in front of him, but there wasn't enough room for him to stand without knocking her back off of her feet.

Amos wrapped his arm around her body and lifted her up with him as he stood.

The sudden lift shocked her. Her eyes widened, and she wrapped her arms around his neck.

When he set her down, she loosened her hold on him, but didn't let go.

And standing there, her gaze on his face, her arms around his neck, Amos lifted the towel and dried her hair.

All he could think about was what it would take to keep her forever.

# CHAPTER SIX

A pril Reynolds knew that it was a crazy set of circumstances that landed her right where she was.

Tucked in bed, literally squished between Amos and his dog, Tank.

She could still remember the blissful look in the dog's eyes as he launched himself up onto the bed. Amos had groaned under his breath just as the bed had when Tank was settled down on one side.

Amos took her hand and helped her up and from that perch on the edge of the mattress, she crawled up to the pillows.

That was the moment things shifted for her.

No, she wasn't thinking about the way Tank's weight on the edge of the bed tipped her in his direction.

She was remembering the look on Amos' face as he stood beside his own bed.

He looked at the mattress and linens as if he was going to an execution.

His.

April just couldn't understand the longing she felt deep

inside her chest, but what she didn't want to do was make Amos feel like he had to tip-toe around in his own home.

A man's home is his castle.

Goodness knows she saw that on enough decorative plaques at Buc-ee's all over the place. Etsy? Yep. Heck, even the 'Zon had cute signs and t-shirts.

She was pretty sure she'd read it in a fortune cookie somewhere.

And she wasn't going to make him uncomfortable after he'd done everything to make her feel good.

Make her feel safe.

"You know," she gave him a smile, "I can sleep on the couch. It's super comfortable. I think I proved that earlier when I crashed on it."

He shook his head. "It's close to all the windows. If someone were to come to the cabin-"

"I don't think we have to worry about that tonight, right?"

God, she really hoped that they didn't have to.

"Amos?"

The idea took the air from her lungs. April put her hand over her heart and felt it pounding against her ribs. "Do you-"

"Aw shit." Amos leaned over and picked up the quilt and blanket, lifting it up, "get under there."

She swallowed and slipped under, watching him carefully as she scooted back against Tank, who barely moved except to blow a heavy, warm breath against her neck.

Then she waited, because she wasn't about to ask him if he was also going under the blankets.

He looked at her strangely, as if he'd never seen her before.

Which was true.

It didn't make it any less... confusing.

"Are you sure you're okay with this?"

She startled because for a moment, she thought that she'd said the words.

This was, after all, his home.

His bed.

And the crazy heater at her back, was his dog.

But it was Amos who'd asked the question. He wanted to make sure that she was okay with him sleeping in his own bed.

"You know," she bit into her bottom lip to stave off a shiver, "you've done everything to welcome me... well, to keep me safe. I feel horrible that I was dumped on you out of the blue.

"I'm not trying to make any more trouble for you, Amos. I'm an adult and goodness knows you can pick me up and probably toss me out the door."

"I-"

"I'm not saying you're going to do it. At least I hope you're not, but right now I'm exhausted." She turned her head and saw Tank open one eye and snap it closed as if she hadn't seen him do it. "Looks like Tank is at least faking it for my sake."

"So..." Amos gave her half a smile, "you're saying we could share the bed... for your sake."

April lifted her hand to her face, not quite hiding her yawn behind it. "I'm too tired to move on my own." She slid down under the covers and laid her head on the pillow. "So, it's up to you," she felt her eyes drifting closed and yawned again, "but I'm probably going to fall asleep before you make your decision."

"That's what you think."

She felt the mattress sink and she heard him grunt.

"Too damn stubborn."

April smiled at his words, but kept her eyes closed. "Talking about me or you?"

She felt the weight of the blanket and quilt settle over her, tugged up to her shoulder.

The added warmth settled her, made her squirm and stretch in the welcoming heat.

"Yeah," she heard his voice, softer than it had been just a few moments ago, "I was talking about you."

April managed a smile.

"But I guess it applies to me, too."

She heard his long exhale as the heat of her surroundings lulled her asleep.

"I would have stayed there, talking myself out of getting in here if you hadn't just... hadn't just laid down."

She sighed and fought off another yawn. "I'll have to remember that."

"Yeah?"

She didn't have to hear him laugh because she felt it, shaking the bed beneath her.

"That if I want you to do something," it was hard to concentrate with the heat at her back and her front, "that I'm going to have to do it first?"

It was so warm.

So delightfully warm.

"April?"

"Hmm?" She managed to open her eyes, just a bit and saw Amos looking at her. "Yes?"

"I'm sorry I'm such a jerk."

She reached out her hand and touched his chest, her eyes drifting to the sight of her fingers against the dark plaid of his shirt. "I don't think you're a jerk."

"No?" He sounded more than amused. "I'm not?"

"No." She smiled and her eyes drifted closed again. "Jerks don't have dogs like Tank."

She heard him laugh. "That's how you know?"

"Of course." April snuggled deeper into the warmth of the bed. "You can tell a lot about a person by their puppers," she yawned and sank deeper into the mattress, "and Tank is a total sweetheart."

She heard Amos grumble under his breath. "Tank is a pain in the ass."

April fell asleep smiling.

## – BIG 'N BURLY DUO 3 –

BAM!

April's eyes flew open and she froze, her eyes and ears searching the world around her.

It was dark.

It was warm.

No one was screaming.

No one was bleeding.

No one was dying.

She was safe.

She was alive.

Then why, she wondered, did she feel as if she was paralyzed by fear?

Her heart pounding in her chest.

Her mind whirling with thousands of horrible pictures and memories she hoped that she could purge from her head.

The feeling of Princess' fur under her hands and cheek, warm and wet with blood.

The memory stole her breath from her lungs and she felt tears coursing down her temples and into her hair.

She felt it as if each cell of her body had suddenly come alive.

"Why?"

She couldn't stop herself from speaking.

Nor could she keep that quavering sob from coloring her question.

WHY?

She mouthed the word, unable to catch enough of a breath to make noise.

"April?"

She heard her name from a million miles away.

Maybe that's where she wanted to be.

A million miles from her own head.

From those horrifying memories.

"April? Hey."

More tears, making her vision swim.

"Hey."

She felt something on her shoulder.

A hand.

She tried to pull away, but couldn't move.

DON'T

She mouthed the word, but it did no good in the silence of her head.

A scream makes no difference if it can't be heard.

DON'T TOUCH

"April, it's me. Amos."

Amos?

Those thoughts, the crazy pattern of flashing lights in her head, and the booming sounds of death, disappeared in a single word.

A single thought.

Amos.

"Can you hear me?"

YES

She swallowed and wanted to lift her hands to wipe away the tears.

She couldn't move them.

She couldn't.

And the tears flowed faster.

"Oh, shit. Come here."

April felt herself lift up, roll to the side and stop against a wall of pure heat and comfort.

"God, April. You're scaring me."

It was Amos.

Yes.

She was alive and warm in his arms, her chin resting on his shoulder, rocking along with him, melting into his heat.

"Shit." He strung together a few more colorful words, but his embrace didn't change.

He didn't grow impatient or try to pull away.

"I should have asked you more questions. I should have found out more about what happened. I guess..."

He eased up on the tight hold he had on her body and let her lie back a little.

The room was nearly dark, but there was enough light from the moon outside in the night sky for her to see the look in his eyes.

Concern, verging on panic.

He didn't deserve that.

Not at all.

And then... he broke her heart.

Broke her heart and put it all back together.

He wiped the tears from her cheek. His thumb swept across her cheek. The rough scratch of calluses only made the sensation more earth shattering for her.

April was used to being the girl who was on the go.

The girl hustling and moving forward.

The girl who stood on her own two feet.

But in that moment, she was the girl protected.

Warm and safe and cared for.

"I should have known to expect this." He pulled her tighter into his embrace.

She wanted to argue with him. To give him the plucky, beaming girl who could handle anything, but it was just too easy to lean into the safe shelter of his arms.

April felt and heard the grumble of his voice vibrating through them both.

"I guess I've been out of the game too long."

She shook her head and felt her lips brush against his neck. "It's not your fault that I'm struggling."

"I didn't do much to help yesterday."

Finally, able to move, she wriggled her arms free and wrapped them around his body. Well, as much as she could.

Amos was kind of like Tank.

He was a big guy.

And she'd always had an attraction for guys that looked like big, burly, teddy bears.

So hugging him back wasn't a hardship of any sort.

"April?"

She rubbed one hand up along his back, enjoying the feeling of his flannel sleep shirt under her palm. "Hmm?"

"Are you okay?"

Sighing, she smiled against his throat. "I'm feeling much better now."

He shifted and she found herself on her side, the moonlight revealing more of his face when she lifted her head. "You sure?"

She thought for a minute.

She wanted to just say she was fine, but there was something inside of her that wanted to tell him the truth.

April just wasn't sure that he wanted to hear it.

After all, she'd been dumped on his doorstep less than a day ago.

"Hey. I think I can *hear* you thinking."

She shook her head and drew in a breath. "That's Tank snoring, I think."

He laughed silently and she did, too.

It was just so strange how easy it was to talk to him. How easy it was to touch him.

To be touched by him.

He lifted a hand and brushed some of her hair back from her face. "And I could see how scared you were when you woke up. Do you want to talk about it?"

"I don't think so." She shook her head a little, but her gaze drifted off into the darkness. "I think I just want to forget it. Put it out of my head. Somehow."

She meant to say it flippantly and laugh it off, but maybe it was a measure of how much she'd been effected that she couldn't.

"What can I do to help?"

Was it just that easy?

He asks and she answers?

If it was, then what would she say?

She closed her eyes and pressed her lips together, trying to think before she could let herself speak.

And Amos didn't make it easy.

His hand stroked down her arm, and those calluses made her shiver and hot at the same time.

Tucked against his body, she soaked up his heat, and under his thick quilt and blanket, she felt like they were even more hidden from the world than just being out in the woods.

They were in a cocoon of sorts.

Just the two of them.

And the massive dog that slumbered on behind her.

As far as she was concerned, they were in their own little world.

April stretched, feeling her body rub against his.

Amos didn't pull away or even loosen his hold on her.

Instead, she felt his hands flatten and flex against her back. The movement shifted her body against his and when she breathed out, she felt her breasts press against this chest.

Her legs parted slightly and he lifted his leg just enough that she felt his thigh press between them.

Oh.

April lifted her eyes and met his powerful gaze.

"You okay?"

She could feel his concern in the way his gaze touched her face and the sound of his voice.

"I'm safe," she grinned softly, "and I'm warm."

Amos moved a hand down to her lower back and with just a little pressure, he pressed her tighter against him.

"And it's getting hotter." She licked her lips and heard a deep growl. "That you?"

"Yeah," he shifted under her and she heard him groan. "That's me."

Leaning into him, April reached one hand down and covered the hard ridge she'd felt pressed against her thigh.

"That's me, too."

"Oh, good." April knew her voice had softened. It made sense since she was only able to manage shallow breaths. "I was hoping that was you, too."

She kept an eye on Amos' expression as she cupped him through the flannel of his pants.

His jaw tightened and she felt him swell under her hand.

"April, is this what you want?"

The light outside the window was brighter. Dawn must be approaching.

She could see his face more with the added light.

His jaw tensed and his eyes darkened as he looked at her.

"I want this," she slid her hand in one direction and then the other, enjoying the subtle responses of his body under her searching hand, "I want your hands, too."

She gasped in a breath as the hand he had on her lower back slipped down and she felt his fingers press between her legs, pushing the back of her borrowed nightshirt against her.

She rounded her lower back, pressing her knees into the mattress and her clit against his thigh.

April struggled against her instinctual need to rock against him. The stress that she'd been under was pushing her to rush ahead and find the release she needed, but she wanted to take her time.

Who knew if he'd let her have him again?

The hand he had on her butt curled into her, drawing her higher on his thigh.

"If you're not careful," she put a hand down on his chest, "I'm going to run out of room on your thigh."

"I'd be okay with that."

She leaned back an inch. He smiled, but it was a tight-lipped smile, he looked like he was struggling a little. "Really?"

"I wouldn't mind having you wrapped around me."

Her lips parted on a sudden, gasping breath. "So you meant it when you asked what you could do to help."

His smile relaxed and she felt his free hand reaching for the hem on the nightshirt he'd lent her. "As long as I know you don't think I'm demanding anything from you. I want you, April. I've been lying here in bed wanting you."

It seemed a little crazy, she told herself. She wasn't this forward... with anyone!

There was something about Amos. Even if he growled more than anything else, she found herself drawn to him like a moth to a flame.

And maybe that's all this might be.

A quick flame while they were alone and waiting for word that she was safe.

Maybe that was it. A workplace romance, of sorts?

Would that be enough?

Was she brave enough to go after what she wanted?

Well, she was about to find out.

"I know," she told him, "If anyone is pushing, Amos, it's me. I feel this... this ache for you. An emptiness." She drew in a deep breath and stretched herself across his body and leaned in.

When her lips were just an inch away from his, she paused. "I want you to fill me up, Amos. I'm not asking for forever. I just really need you."

With one hand on her ass, he moved the other to the nape of her neck. "Then get ready, April. I'm going to give you what you need."

# CHAPTER SEVEN

He really hoped that he was talking a good game.

Having April's thighs wrapped around his leg had him good and hard.

Her breasts pressed against his chest? Sent blood rushing south, too.

When he pulled her down to him, his hand on the back of her neck, he hoped that he didn't pass out from lack of blood flow to his brain.

Then her lips touched his and fuck, all other thoughts fled.

It wasn't just that it had been an age since he'd kissed a woman, he knew that nothing could compare to the touch of her skin against his.

One touch, one brush of their lips against each other, and that was all it took. She squeezed her thighs around his and leaned into the kiss, her hands traveling up his chest to land on his face.

She wasn't meek or even gentle.

April held his face while she slanted her mouth over his. Neither of them felt all that practiced, but they were sure making up for any lack of recent experience with hunger and desire.

Amos lost himself in that kiss until she curled her back to climb a little higher on his thigh.

That was when he felt a white-hot flash of pain.

Her knee had nearly made him a eunuch, but she didn't seem to notice, kissing him like she was trying to steal the very breath out of his lungs.

And she had, in a way.

But the pain didn't last long.

Neither did the affect.

He let go of the nape of her neck and moved his hands down to her hips, smoothing his palms over the flannel covered swells and lifted her bodily off of his leg.

Amos felt and heard the gasp of breath against his lips and when he set her down with her knees on either side of his hips, he didn't have to press her close.

April rolled her hips against him and he felt her heat against his dick.

He opened his mouth on a moan and her tongue slipped in.

Her taste was addicting and it felt like she was trying to climb inside of him.

If only that was possible.

He understood the feeling, because he couldn't help how much he wanted inside of her too.

Amos tugged up the hem of the sleep shirt that he'd put on her in the bathroom and when it was high enough, he palmed the sweet curves of her ass.

He dug his fingers in as she rocked against him and he heard her groan as her hips ground against his.

She went right back to kissing him as he dragged her up

just enough that he could reach one hand over her amazing ass and slide the tips of his fingers through her sex.

April was wet, and the sweet slide of her liquid heat between his fingers made him nearly mad with desire.

He'd promised to fill her up and with as hard as he was, that wasn't going to be a problem.

When she rocked back, seeking more of his touch, she nearly blew his mind.

The delicious weight of her on his cock, the friction of their bodies against each other, he felt pre-cum drip down on his belly.

Amos turned his head to the side. "Babe, wait. Stop." He felt her still and wished that there was another way... different words that he could use.

The shock in her eyes was one thing.

Then he saw her physically start to withdraw from him.

Heaven help him if she tried to deflect or apologize.

He didn't think she should, but he swore he saw it coming into her eyes.

"We need to talk before this goes any further."

April shifted back, sitting up. She started to move off of his erection, but he moved his hands from where they where and landed on her hips.

"Let me explain *before* you pull away, okay?"

He knew he might regret this later, but the last thing he wanted was for her to regret it. She'd opened up to him. She'd been upfront with her wants and needs and he didn't want her to regret that.

He wanted to give her a damn standing ovation for letting him see and feel her passion.

She nodded, but he didn't miss how she wrapped one arm across her body.

Something he didn't draw attention to.

"I haven't been with anyone in... years, April. So I need you to know that I don't have... I don't have any protection here." He let one hand drop off her hip to cover her hand where it laid on her thigh. Amos gave it a gentle squeeze. "I'm going to give you that release. I'm planning to do it at least a couple times before that hibernating bear on the edge of the bed decides he's hungry. I'm just going to have to use my hands."

He let go of her hand and swept it up her thigh, taking the hem of the sleep shirt with it.

And when it reached her hip, his hand slipped under the shirt and his fingers teased the silken curls that he'd seen before when he'd dried her off.

He saw the flare of desire in her eyes again and as he moved his thumb between her legs, he saw her fingers dig into her thigh.

April's chin lifted and her back arched and there-

"Oh, god."

He rubbed his thumb against her clit again and her lips parted. He lost sight of her eyes, but he could see the soft purple pre-dawn light highlighting the press of her nipples against his sleep shirt.

Fuck.

Amos wanted to get his hands and his mouth on those breasts.

He'd already seen them, but now, with the soft flannel cupping her like a second skin, he was heartbeats away from cumming like a teenage boy all over his belly.

She looked like a goddamn pinup straddled over his hips.

"That okay with you, babe? You gonna let me make you come on my fingers?"

Before she could answer, he twisted his wrist and slid his fingertips through her folds while his thumb circled her clit.

She rose up a little like she was posting in a saddle. She looked magnificent above him and with the extra space for his hand, he rubbed his fingers into her sex, coating them with her heat.

"Oh..."

She lifted up again and he lifted two fingers under her. When she sat back down, her sex stretched around his fingers.

He smiled as she groaned, rolling her hips forward against his thumb.

This wasn't going to be it for him.

Amos knew that.

No matter how long he had with her, he would make the most of their time and keep those memories alive when she left.

"You're so damn beautiful."

And she was.

The hard press of her nipples against his shirt, her hair falling back from her shoulders and her fingers digging into her thighs.

She looked like a goddess and the edges of his vision darkened a little as her movements rubbed his shirt against his cock.

He pushed his other hand up and under the hem of her shirt and felt his way from her belly to her ribs and finally to her breast.

Oh, shit.

He'd seen her gorgeous breasts, but feeling one in his hand? He felt like he held one of the golden apples of Aphrodite. Unseen, he caught her nipple between two fingers, pinching, pulling, and twisting at that tender morsel.

He wanted to taste it too, but it was cold and the last thing he was going to do was subject her to the chill in the air just so he could have her in his mouth.

Later, he told himself. Later, if he could get her under him, under the blanket, he'd keep her warm and taste every inch of her.

But at the moment, he was trying to give her that first taste of bliss. And he'd get a taste of her on his hand.

"Oh... yes."

Her fingertips were biting into her thigh, creating pale halos in her bare flesh.

Amos felt the walls of her sex grip tighter on his fingers, as if she was trying to hold him in. As hot as her flesh was, as glorious as it would be to let her hold him there, he wanted to feel her muscles convulsing around his fingers.

He lowered his hand from her breast and smiled when she whimpered, missing the stimulation of his fingers.

But he knew he was going to give her something better.

He set his hand on her hip, this time under her shirt. He tutored her with that hand, showed her how to ride his hand and how to deepen her frantic movements.

And when she was near mindless with passion, he murmured her name, trying to reach her through the haze.

He wasn't sure she could hear him through the panting breaths from her lips.

"April, baby. Look at me."

Her eyelids lifted and her gaze fixed on his.

"That's right, April. Let me see you come."

She opened her mouth to speak and he was sure that she was about to tell him that she wasn't quite there.

Well, maybe she wasn't.

Amos curled his fingers inside her body and his fingertips brushed up against a part of her sex with a different texture than the rest.

He stroked along the wall again and smiled.

April's eyes widened in surprise and her jaw dropped as her head fell back.

The movement thrust her breasts forward and he could only dream of another day when he could see her bare, riding him to completion.

And then she sat up, her hands moving restlessly over her body.

She looked lost.

She looked radiant.

"You're so beautiful."

Her eyes fixed on his again. "You make me feel beautiful."

Thank fuck.

He held out his hand to her. "Come here." She didn't move at first. Her eyes were bright, but she looked exhausted. "Let me hold you."

She sank bonelessly to his chest and he turned, putting her back between his body and Tank. When she settled with her head on his chest and arm wrapped around his waist, he gently worked his hand free and brought it up to his lips.

Amos put those fingers in his mouth, sucked and licked them clean as he memorized the taste of her.

As April faded back off to sleep, she groaned and pushed against his chest with her hand.

"I can't believe you just did that."

"Did what?" He felt her shake her head against his chest, and the friction felt damn good. "Taste you?"

"Yes." She snuggled closer and he chuckled, almost bouncing her cheek off of his chest. "Why?"

"Because you taste like dessert, honey." He settled the blanket around her. "And I can't wait taste you on my tongue and have your sugar on my beard."

She couldn't believe it, or so she said. He just drew her close and rubbed her back until she went back to sleep.

# CHAPTER EIGHT

Dan's promise of a day or two came and went.

A week went by.

Then another.

April couldn't help but wait for that shoe to fall and ruin her happy little hideaway.

It was crazy, she knew.

Amos was basically a hermit when she was dumped on his doorstep, but he came out of his shell pretty quickly.

It didn't hurt that once they'd started putting their hands on each other, things just kept going.

That, and Tank had taken to her from the moment he'd caught her scent.

Amos trusted Tank's instincts and from there, well...

April grinned and lifted the comb that she'd found in the box of supplies that Amos pointed out.

Tank was looking out of the enclosed back porch, watching as Amos walked around his property looking for game or any signs that they'd had visitors.

"So, what do you think, boy? I think we can get more of this coat detangled, hmm?"

Tank didn't react to her words, but she doubted that he hadn't heard her.

No.

Amos' dog was just like the rest of his breed, so damn smart. He didn't acknowledge anything he didn't want to. Maybe he didn't like the idea.

Just like the other morning when he didn't want to get out of bed, but Amos knew that his dog needed to go outside and *take care of business.*

But Tank had his head on her chest and she had been playing with the dog's ears, stopping when Amos told Tank to go outside.

Tank just lay there and closed his eyes as Amos urged him to get up.

He even gave a great big sigh as Amos tipped his head back and glared at the ceiling.

April had no doubt that Tank knew what Amos was saying. Every other day he'd gotten up and gone out the bedroom door.

Not that morning.

Not when he'd decided that he liked his head on her chest.

It was just hard to be upset at the big fluffy dog when she loved him like her own.

He was, she noted, the first dog who she'd spent any real time with. Nights, mornings, and all the cuteness in between.

"Okay."

She grinned, happy that Tank felt comfortable enough with her at his back to just stare out into the winter wonderland outside the cabin.

"Let's give this a try again, hmm?"

She tucked the comb into the breast pocket of her shirt.

Well, Amos' shirt. It wasn't safe to go to the nearest town

for clothes and the last thing she wanted to do was open up any of her online clothing accounts and have something shipped.

So, Amos had lost some of his flannel to her.

April moved her hands over Tank's thick coat and combed her fingers through the parts that she'd already detangled. She went back through and massaged her fingertips into his muscles in those same areas, and Tank melted against her touch.

"Like that? Feels good not to have tangles everywhere, huh?"

He huffed at the suggestion as if saying 'duh.'

"Well, once we've worked all of these tangles out, it'll be easy to maintain. Then we'll just have to brush out the dirt that gets on the surface and after winter is over, we'll watch out to see when you start blowing your undercoat and we'll get some of my tools and-"

Her hands slowed on his back as she remembered that this wasn't a permanent thing.

She wouldn't be here when Tank started shedding his winter undercoat.

April had no idea that her hands had stilled completely until she felt Tank's cool nose against her arm.

The chill of his touch made her jump a little and she put on a brave face. "Sorry, boy. Did I stop and ruin your fun?" She reached for the comb in the pocket of her shirt and started to work through the tangles along his flank.

Tank seemed to go from a solid to a semi-liquid state as he melted down to the ground.

When he tried to roll on his back to bare his belly, she shook her head and laughing, she gave him a nudge. "No rubs until we finish up this section."

Tank didn't grump and he didn't whine, he just laid there before her and let her work through his coat.

"You know, I always thought I wanted a husky dog."

Tank opened one eye and looked at her.

"Wanted. Past tense."

His eyes closed and she continued to work with the comb at his tangles.

"But after this, I know I've changed my mind."

Tank's side lifted and dropped like a bellows and she smiled even more.

"I've groomed my share of them and I thought, because I could manage the drama during the grooming that I'd enjoy that kind of energy at home.

"You've changed that." She swallowed at the lump she felt in her throat. "I think about all of that frenetic energy and I get tired just thinking about it."

Clearing another part of his coat, she moved on.

"I love your energy, you big pupper fluff butt."

Tank blew out a breath through his nose and stretched out a paw to push at her leg.

"Aww, sweetie." She leaned in and wiggled her fingers through his coat around his neck. "You like me, too?"

It was easy to smile for Tank. Tank made everything easy.

"I love your calm." She continued working on the tangles. "I think you could have been named Zen. Or Monk. You don't seem all that fearsome to me."

She knew they were great guard dogs. Half of the fun of becoming a dog walker before she became a dog groomer was learning the differences between the breeds and what was normal and what was just bad behavior.

A lot of people paid tons of money to have their pretty puppies walked and didn't bother training them or continuing to train them, and that made for misbehaved puppers.

She had to learn to work with those 'trouble children' who deserved just as much love as every other dog. It wasn't their fault that they were spoiled by their parents.

In fact, she'd overheard some early education teachers in a cafe talking about the problems they were having with children whose parents didn't believe in rules and consequences.

If she hadn't known they were teachers, she could have easily seen them as dog walkers. The problems were the same. Even the successes. You could only take care of them when they were in your sphere of control.

One or two of her most challenging puppers just yo-yoed back and forth between good behavior and... what they got away with at home.

"But you're a good boy, Tank."

His mouth opened and his tongue lolled out.

Yeah, he understood what they were saying to him.

"You're smart, too. Right, boy?"

He lifted his head a little, making eye contact with her before he laid back down and let her work on his coat.

"So smart that I bet you know I'm going soon, right?"

She blinked at the sudden tears in her eyes and turned her head away, looking back at the door that would take her back into the cabin.

Closing her eyes, she drew in a steadying breath and let it go.

She was a big girl who didn't have more than the big girl panties that she came with. But she had them in the dryer. So she could cry a little now and pull them up later.

"Okay, buddy. Let's get this done so we can show your daddy how you look when your coat looks like a million bucks. Then maybe he'll hire me and I can come back and visit."

Right.

Yeah.

She knew it would be a long shot.

After she left and went back to her life, she'd be a couple of hours away and her little van wasn't exactly built for roads in this forest.

That she knew for certain.

When Dan had driven her out to Amos' cabin there had been times when she thought her teeth might rattle right out of her head from all of the pits in the road.

Not to mention the unpaved drive up to the cabin.

Unable to grab the 'oh shit' bar above the door, she'd made do grabbing the hand rest in the door itself.

Her van, if it had made it through the pitted road, would have died from sheer fright as soon as her wheels hit the driveway.

So, no. She wasn't coming back once she left.

Until then, she could allow herself to think that she belonged there.

That fantasy helped her feel safe. It gave her hope.

And that was what she had to concentrate on.

When Amos came back, she was lost in thought. Well, lost in trying to figure out what to cook for dinner. Amos did a lot of the cooking since he was familiar with the supplies and why he'd bought them, she just wanted to do something for him.

Especially since he'd spent most of the day walking around the woods and she'd just stayed in doing... what she'd been doing for weeks.

She'd finally decided on putting together some beef patties that they could turn into other meal components for the next few days.

It made sense.

It helped take the busy work out of their daily life.

She heard the back door open and she spoke over her shoulder. "I'm putting something together for dinner. Go ahead and get warm by the fire."

She hoped that he took her at her word and sat down. Hell, she hoped that he put his feet up for a while.

April heard him hang up his coat on a hook in the hall, but she didn't hear his boots on the floor.

"What happened to your boots? Did you leave those outside?"

The door to the bedroom opened and she rolled her eyes. He was doing things out of order and while that was a little confusing, she was sure it was driving Amos a little nuts.

He liked his routine.

And she liked watching him do his routine.

When the door opened up, she saw him look up and smile at her.

"Hey, gorgeous."

Her heart melted all over again.

"Hey, handsome."

He adjusted the shirt he'd just changed into and she turned back to the counter, chopping the onions she'd taken out of the storage area.

Amos walked up beside her and then backed up a few steps.

April looked at him with a curious smile. "Something wrong?"

He shook his head. "No. Everything was good on my walk."

She nodded. "Right. I know that or you would have rushed in here and been all business." She looked down as she diced a slice of the onion and then she looked back at Amos who was leaning back away from her.

"Usually, you come in and give me a kiss."

He didn't move.

"At least on the cheek."

Still no movement.

"Amos?"

He gestured at the cutting board. "I'm good right here."

"Ah..." She turned back and moved the next slice from the pile and onto the cutting board in front of her. "You don't like onions."

"No." His voice was stronger, almost a little too strong. "I like onions. I eat them."

She narrowed her eyes at him. "But I've never seen you cut them." That's when it hit her. "That's why you're staying that far away. You don't want to cry."

"I'm okay with crying." He folded his arms across his chest and leaned his hip against the counter. "I just don't want to do it if I don't have to."

She shrugged, but he continued on as if he had something to explain.

"It's not like I'm afraid of it."

She had to hold back a chuckle. "Of course not. There are a lot of things that I'll go out of my way not to do, so I understand."

"A lot of things like..."

"Like..." It took her a moment to pick something out of the list. "Like spiders. If I'd seen one when I walked into your cabin, I would have gone right back to the car with Dan and made him take me somewhere else."

"You could have gone in the car, April, but you wouldn't have left with Dan."

April looked up at Amos and her shoulders shook with laughter.

"No, I wouldn't have. I felt safe here." She slid the next slice off of the pile. "But if I see a spider now, I'm going to insist that you kill it. Kill it dead. Or burn down the house."

It was his turn to laugh. "I'll take care of you, don't worry."

She nodded. "I know."

"So," he leaned to the side to take a look at her set up, "what's the secret to keeping the onion from burning your eyes?"

"Secret?" She shook her head. "Nothing like that."

He crossed one leg over the other with a, "Huh. So, you're telling me it's... magic?"

She laughed out loud and from his place beside the open fireplace, Tank lifted up his head and howled just a little, laughing in his own way.

"Nope," she tried to assure him, "no magic."

She finished dicing the slice in front of her and used the flat of the knife blade to move it to the side before dropping another on the cutting area.

"I learned early on that I wasn't like most people when it came to onions. It didn't really make me cry, or even tear up.

"In Home Ec class in middle school almost everyone else in the class, including my teacher, was more than a little jealous. After all of the people on my team had proved our knife skills to the teacher, I spent the rest of the classes that semester gladly chopping onions whenever we needed them for a recipe.

"It was nice to be different in a good way. Usually at that age when you stand out it's because you had toilet paper stuck to the bottom of your shoe or fell flat on your face in the cafeteria. It was the difference between been 'famous' for something good instead of infamous for being a mess.

"Until the start of the next semester, after Winter Break." She paused and set her knife down. She wasn't afraid that she'd tear up, but talking about this probably wasn't a good thing to do with a sharp knife around her fingers. "Haley Masters heard someone joking in the hallway about how she'd balled like a baby in Home Ec class from the onions. And then someone else piped up and said that I could have done with no problem what-so-ever.

"Well, as soon as someone noticed that Haley was in the hallway, it seemed like the whole school went silent."

April took a steadying breath and rushed on to finish the story. She didn't want to dwell on it or she just might start crying even if it was stupid looking back on it.

"She stomped right up to me and pushed her hand against my shoulder."

*"So you think you're so damn cool."*

"It sounded like everyone in the hallway gasped and then went dead silent. Cursing in school would get most people suspended." She looked up at Amos and saw that he was listening intently to her story.

"Most people," he canted his head to the side, "meaning everyone but Haley?"

She smiled. "You catch on fast."

"It's about you," he smiled. "I pay attention."

That warmed her just as much as his kiss would have.

"Well, I kept my hands to myself because Haley's dad was a lawyer and her mother was a raving narcissist. If I'd put one hand on her, I shudder to think what would have happened to me. So I just stood there.

"That made her even more mad."

Amos shrugged. "Sounds like she would have been more mad, no matter what."

"Another point for the hot guy in flannel."

He smiled and looked around the room behind him, before turning back to her and pointing at his chest. "Me?"

She rolled her eyes. "You know it's you."

"And you with that knife in your hand when I walked in is pretty damn sexy, too."

She raised an eyebrow at that. "Kinky, much?"

His smiling shrug made it easier to finish the story.

"Her fingers curled and looked like claws and there I was afraid that she'd take a swipe at my face or something, but she didn't use her hands, she used her words."

April felt the skin on her face prickle with heat and her stomach twisted up inside of her.

"It'll probably sound so stupid now, but back then it felt worse than a slap. It felt like she'd clawed open my chest and left a gaping hole there."

*"Well, only people with hearts can cry, so you... You're just a heartless bitch!"*

April waited for the pain to knife through her chest like it had so many years ago, but it didn't hit so hard now.

With a sigh of relief, she looked at Amos. "Wow. The last time I even thought about that story, I cried for hours. I guess I've grown up, huh?"

"I think you've been grown up for a long time, April. I think the difference is that you're believing in yourself now. You don't think I've noticed how you carry yourself? You went through hell and you've only become stronger."

"You know just what to say to make me smile."

"I'm telling you what you need to hear. Giving you the recognition that you've earned."

"Still," she gave him a pinched lip grin, "all of that build up I gave it and then *pfft*." She turned back to the counter and went back to chopping. "It was a stupid story."

She should have known that Amos wasn't going to let it go.

"Hey now, careful with that knife." She heard him coming up behind her and felt him set his hands on her hips.

It was only one of the places that she liked to have his hands.

She managed to continue chopping because she knew that she was going to be distracted very, very soon.

April felt his chest against her back and then his lips against the back of her neck. She swallowed and waited until he broke the contact before she finished, rushing a little more than she should.

"I thought you didn't want to be near the onions." She heard a little edge of cheek in her voice and smiled, realizing that Amos was right about that, too. She was stronger. She was different.

And she was damn proud of it too.

"Sure, I still hate onions, but you're worth the danger."

Worth the danger.

It reminded her about why she was there.

She was in danger.

And Amos was going to put himself between it and her if the time came.

A sacrifice she didn't think she could agree with.

"Hey," Amos pressed a kiss to her temple and whispered into her ear, "something wrong?"

What wasn't wrong?

"Babe-"

"How can you stand to have me here?" April hated the pitch of her voice, a little too high for her own ears and scratchy with emotion. "You go from living your life to putting your life on the line for me. You didn't know me from Adam before this. How can you smile at me? Kiss me?"

"Put the knife down."

He pressed against her back and nipped her earlobe with his teeth.

She put the knife into the sink and saw that her hands were shaking just a little.

Amos swept his tongue against her ear to soothe the sting.

How could she be wet from just that?

Well it wasn't just that.

It was Amos, and she could feel his beard against her neck.

She really loved that beard.

He kissed her neck and she grabbed the edge of the counter, her hips pushing back against him.

She was so tired of thinking about all the wrong things. She wanted to feel all of the good things.

And that meant Amos Kane touching every inch of her body.

He wrapped an arm around her middle and pulled her back against him.

If she thought she was wet before, she was wrong.

*Now*, she was wet.

And needy.

Amos braced his hand on the counter beside hers and, with his hand on her belly, he pressed against her harder, bending her over.

The feel of his cock pressed hard against the tops of her thighs, cushioned against her ass. She knew she needed him sooner rather than later.

"Amos?"

"Yeah?"

She looked over her shoulder and caught his eye. "Here."

His eyebrows lifted a little. "Here?"

April nodded. "Here."

"All right." Amos disappeared out of sight, and she didn't know where he'd gone.

Before she could turn around to look, she felt one of his hands on the back of her thigh and then the hem of her sleep shirt lifted, baring her completely.

"Hold on to the counter, April."

What else could she do but comply?

# CHAPTER NINE

Amos had been feeling an itch in the back of his neck since he woke up that morning. It wasn't an easy feeling.

In fact, it made him more than a little nervous.

He hadn't felt like that in a long, long time, but as he moved around the house, double and triple checking the locks and yes, the safe, he chalked it up to the feeling of walking on eggshells around April.

The night before, when he was just about to fall asleep, he heard her whisper, "I love you."

Fuck.

He wanted to say it first.

Even worse, he'd been tongue tied after hearing her say it. So stunned that she'd been asleep before he managed to make a sound.

That didn't sit well with him, because he didn't want her to think he didn't share those feelings.

He shook his head while he was waiting for the coffee machine to do its job and mentally kicked his ass.

Amos was going to tell her that he loved her, but now he

felt like he had to make a thing about it. Just saying it would feel like he was just echoing her words and April deserved better.

April deserved all the bells and whistles.

And...

He blew out a pent-up breath.

He was hoping that she wanted to stay.

That was part of the problem.

She had her job. She had her clients.

All of that was hours away. In another fucking city.

It might as well be in another state.

And he didn't really know if he wanted to... people again.

Her? Absolutely.

Other people.

He sighed.

He'd do it for her.

"Amos?"

He felt her hand against his chest the very moment he heard her voice and with that shock came a reaction he hadn't expected.

In a heartbeat, he had her wrist in his hand and her arm twisted behind her back.

"Amos! What-"

Shit!

He let her go like she was hot metal, burning him.

Only it was his action that was burning. Burning him with shame.

"Aw, shit! April, are you okay?"

She rubbed at her wrist gently and he had a feeling she was doing it that way to make him think it was okay.

"April, I'm... I'm sorry." He reached for her wrist, but her eyes widened just a hint and he lowered his hand away. "I thought, no. I didn't think. I was-"

"Hey." She gave him a smile, but it wasn't as full as her normal smile. "I get it. I surprised you and you... You're trained to react."

"To danger," he clarified. "I'm trained to react to danger."

"I should have thought about it first," she continued to bring the guilt on herself, "but you looked like you were a little lost in thought."

"I was." He answered too quickly. Jumping on the excuse. "I would never hurt you."

He shook his head. He was already a liar in that capacity.

"Intentionally," she smiled. This time that smile reached her eyes. "You wouldn't hurt me intentionally. I know that, Amos."

He was still frustrated at himself, but he still had that feeling itching at the back of his neck.

"The coffee should be ready soon," he tried to lighten the look on his face, "but while we're waiting, I want you to walk me through the plans we worked out."

Amos saw the shadow that crossed her features, but he wasn't going to be swayed by it.

"April, please."

Tipping her head back, she sighed. "I would really love some coffee first."

He reached out and took a hold of her forearm on the same arm that he hurt. Lifting it carefully, he turned it side to side so he could see her wrist.

There was the hint of a bruise forming on the inside of her wrist, near her pulse.

The sight made him sick to his stomach.

"Just tell me what you remember, April. Please."

He watched her square her shoulders and fix a smile on her face.

"If someone comes who you don't recognize or someone

you think could be trouble. I go to the linen closet." She pointed to the door opposite the pantry. I open the door and push the shelves in. They'll lock into place like steps and that will take me through the panel in the ceiling."

"And in the ceiling?"

"Well, it's the loft up above and there's a nook where I can fit into a false wall in the bricks of the chimney. I stay there until you give me the all clear."

He nodded. Almost satisfied.

"And the all clear?" He wanted to hear it from her.

"Come here, girl." April rolled her eyes. "I'm not a dog."

"No," he opened his arms and she stepped into his embrace, "you're not. But that's why it's the all clear. If there's someone here who's trying to get to you, they'll make me call for you.

"And nothing I would say should bring you out of hiding except something that would make no sense to anyone else, but us."

"And confuse the hell out of Tank in the process."

She leaned her cheek against his chest and he felt breathless.

"You know, I hate that you had to go through everything you did at the Helm's house."

April shrugged.

"But I love that it brought you to me."

She leaned back, a quizzical look on her face.

For a moment, he wondered if she'd heard the word 'love' and thought about what he might be saying.

He let out a breath and smiled, knowing that this might be just the right moment to talk to her. "April."

"Yeah?"

He saw her smile and damn, she looked gorgeous.

"I wanted to talk to you about something."

She turned to him and put her hands on his chest, licking her lips to wet them.

It made them super kissable. Not that he had any trouble wanting to kiss her on the regular.

"I-"

They both stopped short, hearing noise outside the front of the cabin.

Before Amos could stop her, April ran to the front windows to look out.

"April!"

She waved him off. "It's Dan's car." She turned her back to the window. "Dan. He's the other agent. Marshal," she corrected, "whatever."

He shook his head as she reached for the door.

"Hey, at least let me make sure he's by himself before you go running outside, okay?"

She moved to flatten her back against the wall between the front door and the bank of windows. "Yes, sir."

He had his hand on the door when she spoke next.

"Is this good, sir?"

Heaven help him. She was a tempting little minx. "Yes. It's very good."

Her laughter did him good too.

"Now, stay here. I'm hoping he's just come to give us the news that they've arrested all of the people involved with the plot against the Helms."

He opened the door and stepped outside onto the porch.

— BIG 'N BURLY DUO 3 —

She heard his boots on the steps and used that as a good clue that he felt safe enough to walk out to the Navigator. Leaning a little to the side, she tried to see around the edge of the window frame.

She could see just enough to know that Amos was approaching the car from the passenger side.

Strange.

She straightened and went back to standing behind the wall.

He was waiting for news that they'd arrested the men responsible.

Did he think it would be good news?

She rolled her eyes heavenward.

It would be, right?

That was the whole reason why Dan had dumped her on Amos' doorstep, to protect her from the men responsible for killing the Helms.

So if they had been arrested, then Dan would take her home.

April pressed the heel of her hand over her heart to ease the sudden ache she felt. That was news, but she wasn't sure it was good news.

But maybe Amos did.

Maybe that's what Amos was going to tell her when they heard Dan coming up the driveway.

She'd told him she loved him the night before.

It was an impulse thing. It was crazy.

She knew it then and still did it.

April wanted to blame it on the orgasmic haze that he'd put her in.

The man was certainly driven to make her happy in bed. On the couch.

And that one time against the kitchen counter.

Okay, so Amos was a generous lover, but maybe that was as far as it went, because when she'd said that she loved him, he was still awake.

She knew he'd heard her.

She'd felt the sudden stillness of his body against hers.

April went to sleep with him lying uncomfortably beside her.

How much of an ass did that make her?

She startled when she heard footfalls on the steps. Amos' booted feet and another pair with softer shoes.

April smiled at the thought that she knew what Amos sounded like when he walked. If this was the day that she was leaving, she had a bunch of memories to take with her.

She stayed where she was when the door opened and she stayed right where she was when Amos stepped inside.

He saw her right away and gave her an amused grin as he waited for Dan to walk in.

Then he closed the door.

"Welcome back."

The FBI Agent whirled around and smiled when he saw her. "Oh good," he nodded, "Amos didn't lose you out in the woods."

She laughed at his joke. "No, not that he didn't try." She shrugged and gave Amos a wink. "I'm like a bad penny. I keep turning up."

April gestured to the coffee pot that had finally gotten its shit together. "Do you want some coffee?"

Dan waved off the offer. "No thanks," he put his hands on his belly, "I drank my weight in the stuff on the way here."

"Okay." April moved past him to pour some for herself and Amos. If they were going to hear news of either kind, she wanted caffeine.

And a lot of it.

Lifting her cup and Amos' from the drying rack, she set them down on the counter and reached for the coffee pot.

"So," she hesitated for a second, tapping the handle of the coffee pot, "what's the news?"

Dan chuckled. "You get right to point, I see. Well, I wanted to let you both know how sorry I was to leave you here all this time.

"I should have called or come up earlier to explain what was going on, but coming here when things were up in the air would have been a bad idea."

She poured the two cups and managed to keep her peripheral vision on him. "You would have led people to me, I get it."

"Yeah," he smiled. "I guess you do."

He turned to Amos as she handed Amos his cup.

"I hope you didn't mind having a roommate for this long, old man."

Amos barely reacted to his words, lifting the coffee cup to his mouth.

The coffee had to be burning hot on his tongue, but still, Amos took a sip.

"So, the good news is that I'm here to take April home."

That 'good' news hit her like a brick. Stunned didn't even begin to cover it.

Dan looked her over from head to toe, and she frowned. What was he looking for? "Looks like you're following the flannel fashion trend. Looks good on you, April."

"Well, it's not like I could take her shopping. She's been a great sport about all of it without a whole lot of help." Amos looked at Dan. "Let's just avoid the whole fashion commentary, okay?"

Dan shrugged and held his hands out in a supplicating

gesture. "I didn't mean anything by it. She looks good, man. This is a time to relax. I'm taking her off your hands."

A muscle ticked in Amos' jaw and April didn't know how to read that.

She wanted to pull him aside and ask him, but the last thing she wanted was for Dan to listen in and make fun of something else.

Having him inside the cabin made her feel like the energy of the house was off.

Strange, right?

Maybe it was just how irritating he was.

It was something she didn't notice when he had her in the car on the way here. She was too busy crouching down out of sight.

And maybe that was a good thing.

"Amos? Hey, I'm going to talk to the boss about getting you some money for doing all of this. It won't be a lot, but it should pay for whatever she ate while she was here. Water usage and stuff."

"You don't need to." Amos' voice sounded quieter than normal and a little hard. "I don't need any money."

April bit the inside of her cheek. She wanted him to look at her and say, "I just need you."

Wishful thinking? Sure.

But she was crazy in love with him.

Crazy being the operative word.

"April?"

She turned to look at Dan. "Yeah?"

"You want to go and get your stuff?"

There wasn't much. She could change into the clothes she had on when she stumbled into the middle of hell, but that was all she really had.

"You can take those with you."

She looked at Amos and saw him nodding at her and she took it to mean that she could take his clothes with her.

"Sure, thanks."

She wondered what he would think if she confessed that she wanted to take them. She wanted something to remember him by when she was hundreds of miles away and missing him.

She pointed at the bedroom. "I'll go and get my things. It will probably make sense to wear my clothes instead of the stuff I was sleeping in. It'll just be a few minutes."

As she walked away, she heard Dan laugh.

"Sharing a bed, hmm?"

Amos didn't say a word.

Somehow that hurt even more.

## – BIG 'N BURLY DUO 3 –

As soon as April left the room, Amos turned on Dan. "Shut the fuck up."

Dan shrugged. "Wow. What happened to you? You're almost... human."

"Shut it, man. This is not the time and she is not the girl you want to lose teeth over."

Dan stared at him. "So it's like that."

Amos got a hold of his shirt, pulling him up to look him in the eye. "Leave it alone."

Lifting his hands in surrender, Dan struggled to compose his expression. "Sorry. Seriously, I'm sorry."

Amos let him go.

"I'm just kind of happy to see you... coming out of your funk, you know?"

Amos took another sip of the coffee, happy to let the pain

on his tongue pull focus away from his irritation with Dan. He had no idea that Dan was so goddamn nosy.

"It's crazy, right? I leave her here for you to watch her and when I come back, you're all white knight."

Twisting his neck, Amos felt something crack in his spine and it felt good.

It was the only thing keeping him from doing the same to Dan's neck.

He heard April moving around in the bedroom and turned away from Dan. He wanted to talk to her before she left, but Dan was too curious by far, and Amos didn't think that April would want him to overhear or get into their business.

"So, what charges were they brought in under?"

He heard a pause and then, "Hmm?"

"The men responsible for the murders."

"Oh, yeah. Look, I actually wasn't there at the take down. I was just sent out here to get April."

Amos let out a pensive breath. He moved over to the counter and set down his coffee cup. He wanted to do something with his hands or he was going to lose his mind.

"I'm going to make some toast so she can take it with her. She hasn't had anything to eat yet." He reached for the bread box on the counter. "You want me to make you some for the road?"

"Toast?" Dan's chuckle was like nails on a chalkboard. "You're going to make us toast?"

Amos felt a muscle tick in his cheek. "That's the idea."

"Well, don't bother."

Amos felt that same prickle of sensation on the back of his neck that he'd felt a little earlier.

The same niggling feeling that he'd pushed away.

In one moment of clarity, he'd realized that he'd overlooked one very important detail.

Amos grabbed for the bread box a second too late.

Blood splattered all over the tin box and then Amos went down to his knees.

# CHAPTER TEN

April had one leg in her pants when she heard the shot.

She froze in place, her heart leaping into her throat.

"Amos." She knew what she'd been told to do if a threat showed up, but suddenly she was rethinking everything.

Amos hadn't called out a warning.

He hadn't seen the danger coming.

That meant that the shot she heard was likely at him.

And the fact that she hadn't heard him call the all clear or anything else, she had to consider that he wasn't able to. To make it even worse, Tank was crouched protectively beside her. He hadn't made a peep when she heard the shot, but she could see that he was ready to pounce the moment he got the chance.

Did Tank know something?

If he wasn't breaking down the door to get to Amos, did that mean—

"Oh god." Her knees went weak but she wasn't going to let them give out. She had to think of a way to help Amos.

Then the bedroom door swung open and standing there, a gun pointed at her, was the very person who'd 'saved' her life before.

"Well, isn't this a pretty sight."

April didn't have to look down to know what he saw.

She was in her bra and panties and one stupid leg of her pants. She wasn't in any position to be a help to anyone.

But she could fake it, right?

Lifting her chin, she looked at Dan. "What did you do to Amos?"

His smile made her sick to her stomach.

"I made him the latest victim of a vicious crime family."

No.

"And you, my dear," he licked his lips, "are going to be next."

April fought back tears. The last thing she wanted to be was a helpless mess.

"Now, why don't you come out here with us and I'll take care of this quickly."

Out there meant she could be with Amos.

She could, at the very least, see him one last time.

If only she could keep Tank hidden away, but there wasn't much that could hide Tank except for his namesake.

"Come on, April. Don't make me wait, or I'll drop you right there and forget making it look pretty."

She hesitated, and he raised the gun from her chest toward her head.

"Let's go."

Angry and likely half-crazy, April reached down and pulled off the one pants leg she managed to get on.

"You look good," he leered at her, "too bad this is going to have to be quick, I need to get all of the pieces in place."

"Yeah," she nodded at him when she wanted to tear him apart, "I'm really concerned with your schedule."

He held the gun out, extending his arm straight at her. "Just get your ass over here."

"Okay." She took a step and called out a command she'd seen Amos practice with Tank. "Go!"

Tank flew through the air, his massive jaws opening just to close around Dan's forearm.

They went down in a mass of fur and human limbs.

She wanted to help the dog take him down for good, but she had to see Amos.

She had to know.

Scrambling over the bed, she ran into the hall and almost straight into the bathroom room.

With her eyes on the main room, she saw everything at once.

"Amos!"

He was leaning against the cabinets under the counter, his shoulder and temple pressed against the dark green doors.

Blood was soaking the front of his shirt and she dropped down to her knees in front of him. "Amos. Amos? Can you hear me?"

His eyelids twitched a little and he drew in a breath that made blood flow from a wound in his chest.

A shot and a howl in the bedroom ended the human screams and April shot to her feet to grab for a knife from the block on the counter.

It wasn't going to be much against a gun and a man trained to kill, but she'd give it a try.

As she reached for the knife, the handle slipped out of her bloody fingers and she reached into the sink to grab it, she saw something else laying in the metal basin.

Something she hadn't expected to find.

"Well, now I'm piss off, April!"

She heard Dan struggling to breathe as he moved out of the bedroom.

"That fucking dog fucked up my arm! So I'm going to have to shoot you with the other one. And for that," he sneered, "I'm going to make it hurt. I'm going to make it slow. And by the time I put one in your head, you're going to be begging for it if you're even conscious enough to beg."

She prayed she remembered the lessons that Amos had given her, because she was going to need that and every ounce of strength she had left in her to do what needed to be done.

"So turn, the fuck, around, so I can kill you!"

Okay.

Her arms moved first.

She grabbed the grip with both hands, safety off, point and shoot.

This close she didn't have to be an expert, she just had to have a target big enough and Dan was right there, just feet away.

It went through his arm and the shot threw him back against the wall, his gun falling from his hand.

"What the fuck?"

She didn't know if he was wearing a bulletproof vest, but that didn't really matter to her in the long run.

Like there was a long run for her anymore.

April planted her feet, raised the gun with both hands, and put a couple of rounds through the front of his pants.

Dan looked down at the mess she'd made, and when he looked up at her again, he had one last message for her. "You. Bitch."

She turned and moved back to Amos and reached into his pocket. She withdrew his phone and fumbled the code that he'd given her.

That's when she remembered she didn't even need the code to dial for an emergency.

Back down on her knees, she yanked the kitchen towel hanging from the drawer pull and pressed it tightly against the bullet wound in his chest.

"Carter Town 911. What's your emergency?"

# CHAPTER ELEVEN

When he came to, he knew he was in a hospital, which was much better than a morgue.

The noise from the machines surrounding his bed sucked rocks.

How anyone could get rest with all of that noise, he had no fucking idea.

His head was pounding, and his thoughts were all jumbled up, but that didn't compare to what felt like a softball sized hole in his chest.

Amos tried to lift his hand to feel around and see the extent of his injuries. He'd been in this kind of a situation before, but this time seemed... worse.

He could barely lift his hand from the bed before he felt something yank his arm back down. It was likely an IV or some such torture device.

Amos felt his lips curve in a snarl to express his feelings.

"Well, that certainly looks like the Amos Kane that I know and love."

Love?

He looked toward the voice and when he saw April's face in his line of vision, everything came back to him.

Well, enough of it.

Dan.

The shot.

The pain and blood.

"You," he spoke and could barely hear his voice, "you're alive."

"Rest your voice, grumpy. I can fill in the holes for you, if you let me."

He stayed right where he was because he couldn't move, but his eyes followed April as she moved to the rolling table along the wall and came back with a cup and a bent straw.

She laughed at him.

"I see that nasty look you're giving this straw, but until you can sit up and drink, this is how you have to do it." April held the cup close enough that he just had to open his mouth and close his lips around the straw. "Good, now while you sip, I'll tell you everything you should know."

He took a sip and saw her smile.

"You're alive. Thank god."

"Tank is almost ready to come home from the vet. He's healing nicely." She reached out and put a hand on his shoulder. "Calm down. If your heart rate goes any higher, I can't stay here with you, and they'd sedate you again."

He forced himself to breathe in and out slowly and listened as the beeping slowed down too.

"After that piece of crap shot you, he came after me and Tank tore his arm apart, but he didn't come out unscathed. Dan shot Tank to get away from him, but our boy ripped his arm a new one."

She held up her hand.

"Yeah, I know, that's not how the phrase goes, but I'm struggling not to weep here, so shush."

"April-"

"I almost lost both of you in one day." Tears streamed down her face. "I wish I could have divided myself in two so I could go with both of you when they had LifeFlight drop down in the back of the house. "I don't think any of them had ever seen a dog like Tank before but there we were the three of us on that helicopter and all I knew is that when you woke up, I was going to beg you to love me, because I love you, Amos Kane.

"I want to go back to the cabin with you and Tank. I want to take care of you and love you and pray that nothing like this ever happens again, because I can't take it."

"Babe-"

"I'm... I'm sorry for crying and being a blubbering mess, but I don't know what else to do. I don't think I can lose you two and survive it."

"April-"

"What!" She drew back in shock and then burst into tears. She hunched over the edge of the bed and dropped her forehead onto the sheets near his fingertips. "I'm sorry. I didn't mean to say that."

"To say what?"

"Yes."

She sniffled and he smiled.

"I think we're in some serious danger of becoming Laurel and Hardy, April. Now, look at me so I can tell you something."

She turned her head, looking up at him with her cheeks streaked with tears.

"That day that I was shot. I was in the kitchen trying to figure out how to tell you two things. One. That I love you. I heard you the night before and I felt like I had to do something to make it special since you'd already beat me to the punch."

"Really?"

He nodded slowly. "Really."

She smiled, but it was a wobbly smile. "And two?"

"Two," he sighed and watched her expression carefully, "I wanted to ask you to stay, or if you needed to testify at a trial, I wanted to ask you to come back with me when it was over.

"I didn't want to let you go, because I love you like crazy."

"Well, I've been crazy these last few days. If it wasn't for your cousin, I don't know what I would have done."

"Vincent? He's been here?"

April leaned over and kissed the back of his hand. "He came to see you, but he and his wife, Lily have been checking in on Tank and sending me updates. The vet is a few blocks away from his shop."

"Wife?"

Smiling at him, April gently took his hand in hers. "He was listed as your Emergency Contact on your medical records, so they contacted him. He'll be by tomorrow with Lily. I think you're going to love her, she's so beautiful."

"You're so beautiful, baby."

For the first time since he'd opened his eyes, Amos drew in a breath that wasn't filled with worry or fear.

He had April at his side.

Tank was on the mend.

And he was alive.

"Wait." He narrowed his eyes at April. "You said Tank tore up Dan's arm, and that he shot Tank, but what happened to him after that?"

April hesitated, but only for a moment. "I went to grab a

knife from the block because I knew I didn't have time to try and get into the safe."

He nodded, listening intently.

"But I dropped the knife in the sink. That's when I saw the gun. I'd forgotten about the gun you keep in the breadbox. I'm just not cut out to be a marshal, I guess."

"Hey." He wrapped his fingers around her hand. "What happened?"

"Well, with his right arm ripped up by Tank, Dan was ready to shoot me with his left. He just wasn't ready for me to pull a gun out of the sink.

"I shot him.

"A few times. And now he's dead and I'm oddly okay with having done it."

"Wow." He shook his head.

"I know, right?" April sounded amazed. "But after what he did to you and Tank, it wasn't hard at all."

"Okay then."

She looked at him with a furrow in her brow. "You're okay with it?"

"Why not? He tried to kill me, and Tank, and you. If he hadn't caught me by surprise, which I might never live down, I was going for that gun to do the same damn thing."

She smiled at him. "So I get to go home with you and Tank."

He smiled back. "And one more."

"One more?"

"Well, I admit that I was getting a little tired of my dog choosing to sleep with you all of the time."

"Tank sleeps with us, Amos."

"He sleeps on your side of the bed and follows you everywhere. And he's my dog."

"Oh, okay. So–"

"I called the breeder who I got Tank from, and he has a female pup almost weened and ready for her forever home. So, if you were willing to stay, I was going to get a dog for you or me, if Tank has abandoned me for good."

April rolled her eyes. "Are you going to be like this with our kids, too?"

"Maybe." He grinned and pulled on her hand so she'd come closer to him. "So I guess we'll just have to make sure we have an even number. Like six."

He loved the shock in her eyes, but she turned it around on him.

"Like... eight?"

"I fucking love you, April."

"And I love you more, Amos."

# ROPED BY THE DAD BOD

# ROPED BY THE DAD BOD

Grayson Brandt was a part of a local rodeo legacy. Not only did the Brandt Family Ranch host the largest rodeo in six states, but he hadn't lost a team roping competition since he'd started entering the competition as a young teen. Coming home from his last rodeo, a drunk driver plowed into his truck, ending his rodeo career, but thankfully not his life.

Since then, he's been healing up at the ranch, leaning on his younger brother to run the ranch, but his recovery has left him a bear. A bear that no one wants to deal with.

The few takers took the job as a housekeeper and light nurse work at the ranch house left within a day, two at the most.

That's when Grayson's brother meets Louise Corning. Louise's daughter had been taking riding lessons at the ranch, but they can't afford it anymore and Louise is looking for a job.

Grayson may be a surly, growly bear, but Louise is a widow and a mom determined to make things work for her daughter.

They might be in a battle of wills, but Grayson soon

figures out that he might not need a housekeeper, but he certainly wants Louise and her daughter to stay on... as family.

How would Louise feel when she'd been Roped by the Dad Bod.

# CHAPTER ONE

## Roped by the Dad Bod

Grayson Brandt stared at the front door of the ranch house and didn't move until he heard the truck in the driveway start up and race down the drive.

He wanted to say that he'd call her later and apologize, but he didn't even know her name. She'd stayed less than four hours as his housekeeper.

A new low record, not that he was proud of it.

On the contrary, he knew he needed help around the house while he fully recovered from the highway accident that had ended his career as a rodeo rider.

He needed the help, but some people just got on his nerves.

Well, six… now seven people.

They didn't understand that things had their places, and he wasn't an invalid. He was almost healed up enough to get around without a cane.

And while he liked having help with meals and such, he really didn't like people in his private space. He didn't like people touching his things.

Sure, he'd been a bachelor for his entire life. Married to

the ranch as his brother liked to tease him. It was a full-time job, seeing to all of the animals, the fences, the supplies. It wasn't for the faint of heart. And it didn't give him much time to court a woman.

Or even go on a date every now and then.

He'd taken the reins running the ranch after their parents passed on and left the living to his brother John. And live John had.

So much so that he was a rodeo champion of his own and married a rodeo queen. They were now taking over the day-to-day chores on the ranch and raising their own cowboys and cowgirls at a home on the other side of the ranch.

It was John who'd hired the first housekeeper. And the second, and third.

The rest had been Laney's doing. She'd tried to find tough as nails people to take him on. The last one could have qualified as a drill sergeant, but she'd crossed the line when she'd gotten out sheers and said it was time to trim his beard.

Oh, hell no.

He'd sent her packing.

There wasn't going to be anyone's hands on his beard except for him. He did a good enough job at it.

Having been responsible for his own grooming since he'd started growing a beard, he knew how he liked it.

The last thing he needed was someone trimming him up crooked or making him look like some fancified city man who smoked Cuban cigars and drank from crystal decanters.

He was a country man and he'd do things his way as long as he was able.

A broken leg may have slowed him down, but it hadn't put him in the ground... yet.

Until it did, he'd do things the right way.

His way.

Grayson heard his phone ring and reached for the cane he'd left leaning against the coffee table and found only air in his hand.

"What the ever lovin'- Fuck!"

His cane was leaning against the counter, a few feet away.

Only too late, he'd remembered that he'd set his cane there as he'd argued with... what's-her-name and he'd hobbled over his armchair and lowered himself into it while he'd given her the verbal boot.

When she'd left, he'd sat there, forgetting to reclaim his cane and now, he might just be a little stuck.

Standing was one thing when he had the cane to lean on, but without it, he'd have to hope that he didn't tip over the armchair getting on his feet.

Or tip the chair over and they'd both be on the floor.

That would just make his day.

RING RING

"Oh, shut up."

He was tempted to let it continue ringing, but then he heard the answering machine pick up.

It was an antiquated old thing, likely from over a decade before, but it worked and it was his, so there it was.

"Gray, it's John. I... I saw Mabel's truck flying toward town, so I'm guessing it didn't work out with her."

"It's not like we were on a date, you yahoo," he grumbled in the direction of the machine.

"Well, while I think Laney's going to be a bit upset, I think I've found you 'the one.'"

"The one?" Grayson sighed and tapped his fingers on the worn armrests of his chair. "What now?"

"I don't know if you remember Jemma Corning. She started riding at the stable last year."

Grayson's lips pursed and he felt his beard scratching

against them as he thought. Picturing the girl was easy enough.

She had a natural seat in a saddle. Western and English, which was rare for a child who hadn't grown up riding. Things came easy for the child, and it wasn't all that easy to find a natural like her.

"Well, her mama's going to show up tomorrow to take care of you. So don't be a total grump or an ass and maybe, just maybe she'll prove you wrong."

"Prove me wrong, huh. Not fuckin' likely." He fisted the hand that would have been on his cane. If only he had the thing, he could throw it at the answering machine.

He'd give the woman a try.

He'd done that for all of the other... failures.

When he let her go, he'd go back to...

"To what?" he asked himself.

"Well," he huffed out a breath as he leaned on the arm of his chair and pushed himself up and out of it, sweating profusely as he did, "I need to get dinner on my table."

The machine hadn't beeped yet, and Laney's voice was heard through the tinny speaker.

"Don't even try to cook something by yourself, Grayson. I'll bring over a warmed casserole for you."

Then he heard the beep and realized that he was, yet again, alone.

"Just like I like it."

His words echoed back at him, and he glared at his reflection visible in the pane of glass beside the door.

"Yeah, right."

## CHAPTER TWO

## Roped by the DAD BOD

Louise Corning was in a bit of a bind. She hadn't told her daughter Jemma exactly what was going on. Mainly because Jemma shouldn't have to worry about things that weren't for little girls.

Okay, she wasn't so little. She was eleven going on eighteen most of the time, but that wasn't something that Louise wanted for her.

Then again, she hadn't expected her husband to die either, but pancreatic cancer didn't ask permission. It appeared suddenly and then it stole Greg's life a little over a year after that, draining their energy and finances along the way.

And since then, she'd done the best that she could.

It turns out that Louise's best wasn't anywhere near good enough and she'd finally had to come to the realization that she couldn't continue her daughter's riding lessons.

They'd paid it up until the end of the school year, meaning that Jemma had her lessons until the end of the month, which was next Saturday.

She thought that had been the end to her troubles.

Well, that would be too easy, wouldn't it?

Two days ago, she'd heard from their landlord. The house that they'd lived in since Jemma had been born was being sold.

And while Mister Roundtree was a kind old man, she understood why he had to sell it. He was going to be in an assisted living center and needed money to pay for it.

That meant she had to find a place to move them within two months.

That was enough bad news, right?

Nope.

The universe decided to deal her another painful blow. The job she'd had for the last five years since she'd gone back to work? They were downsizing the company, and her job was one of the cuts they were making.

They would give her a severance check for a month, given that they felt bad for her. A widowed, single mother wasn't something they wanted on their conscience, her manager had explained.

That had almost been enough to drive her to her knees, but as she'd been sitting in the stands watching Jemma ride around the arena, she'd mumbled to herself. *"God will only give you what you can handle."* Then, with a loud exhale, she looked up at the sky and laughed. *"Well, God... careful, I'm getting really close to the edge."*

That's how she met Laney Brandt.

The woman had sat down beside her in the stands, and they'd talked while Jemma had her lesson with Laney's husband, John.

Not one to whine or complain, especially to people she didn't know, Louise found herself struggling not to cry as she explained the horrible chain of events in her life that had left her wondering how she was going to take care of her daughter during summer break, find a job, and a place to live, all at the same time.

One was hard enough, but all three seemed like an insurmountable problem on her own.

She'd been without Greg for a year, but it felt like an age. The only thing that had lifted Jemma's spirits were the horses, which is why she'd done her best to continue Jemma's lessons for as long as she could.

"I don't suppose you need someone to muck out the stalls in exchange for lessons?" Louise hated how she sounded.

She had no problem doing things for others, but asking for something?

It made her sick to her stomach.

Still, she'd asked because she wanted to try to give her daughter something to look forward to.

Laney Brandt had given thought to the idea. Louise was thankful for that kindness, but she wasn't under any assumption that Laney would be able to help them.

Everyone needed to make money, that fact was impossible to ignore.

"Maybe not mucking out the stalls, but I might have another idea."

Louise clasped her hands together, silently praying that there might be an answer to at least one of her troubles. That might be what she needed to turn their lives around. "Anything."

"Anything?" Laney's wincing smile didn't deter Louise in the least. "How are you with cooking and cleaning?"

"I do it all the time." She felt her heart pound against her ribs, hoping that there might be a lining to the storm cloud above her head. She didn't need it to be silver, just something other than dark would be a lifesaver.

"I don't know if you remember Grayson. He taught Jemma's class a few months ago."

Louise managed to keep her expression still.

She remembered Grayson quite a bit.

In fact, she'd wondered where he'd gone.

She admired the way he worked with the children in the class. Smiled at the way he taught them responsibility and how to care for their horses and tack. And she'd certainly noticed his figure.

She'd been told that everyone had a type. But she called that into question when she'd seen Grayson. He wasn't like Greg who'd been six foot six and skinny as a rail for the entire time she'd known him.

Grayson was built like a bear. Broad shoulders, big muscular arms, and full beard where Greg had barely needed a shave more than once a week or so.

And yet, Grayson had reminded her what it felt like to be a woman. The way her body had reacted to his told her that she was still... alive.

But there was no way she would ever attract his interest.

That didn't bother her in the least.

She was happy drinking in her fill of his barrel chest and thick denim-encased thighs.

Louise shook herself free of her thoughts and looked up at Laney, hoping that the other woman hadn't noticed anything wrong.

It all seemed fine. Laney was smiling at her, an easy smile that was filled with her sunny personality.

"Yes. I remember Grayson. Is he... Is he okay?"

Laney's expression changed then. The corners of her mouth drew down and her posture dropped just a little. "Grayson's truck was hit on the highway on the way back from the Tri-State Rodeo."

Louise felt sick. She covered her mouth with her hands as her heart struggled to understand. "How badly was he injured?"

Laney blew out a breath. "His leg was broken." She touched her hand to her own leg midway from her knee to her hip and Louise had to swallow down the acrid taste of bile from the back of her tongue. "He's on the mend now, but John's taken over most of the day-to-day work on the ranch."

Looking out across the arena, Louise nodded. "He's really good with Jemma. I'm thankful for his help. I... I feel so bad for Grayson, though. You said he's on the mend?"

Laney nodded. "He's too stubborn not to be, but that's kind of where I'm thinking we could use your help."

"Oh? What do you need?" She wasn't sure what she could do with the added load on her shoulders, but she'd do her best to try.

"Grayson needs some help around the ranch house. Basic cleaning stuff. Meals. Things like that."

That sounded like quite the time commitment, but before she could explain her hesitation, Laney spoke again.

"It's a live in position, Louise. You could stay there with Jemma while you're helping Grayson. John can continue to teach Jemma here at the ranch this summer. And you'll have a salary, because believe me, you'll earn it."

Louise couldn't believe what she was hearing.

It was literally the best possible news she could hear.

Just moments before she was wondering how she'd manage to take care of her daughter without a place to live or a job for money and now she could do this job and give her daughter access to the lessons that brought her out of her shell after they'd lost her dad.

"When do I start?"

"How's about tomorrow?"

Louise bowed her head for a moment to say, 'Thank you,' and then she met Laney's gaze with her own. "Perfect. Tomorrow is perfect, thank you."

Now, she had some kind of hope for the future.

She just had to prove herself to Grayson.

## CHAPTER THREE

### Roped by the Dad Bod

The next day she showed up bright and early, ready to work. She'd already fed Jemma at home, having spent the night before packing up their things.

It wasn't much, but the boxes she'd packed would stay in the living room, just inside the door until she got permission to store them at the ranch.

It wasn't something she wanted to ask on the first day. She didn't want to sound like she was marching in and taking over.

And she certainly wasn't going to take Jemma over to the ranch house until she'd found out which room they'd be sleeping in from Grayson.

She had a feeling that he wasn't going to be all that excited to see her. It was the way that Laney talked about him. She was hesitant but hopeful, which Louise took to mean that there would be a challenge.

She was ready for it.

This wasn't just playing house. She needed a place for herself and her daughter to stay while she figured out where they would go before the next school year started.

Thankful that John was keeping Jemma with him at the

stables and showing her the ropes of taking care of all the barn animals on the property, Louise had driven across the ranch to the main house.

It looked like love had lived there for years. The whole house gave her a feeling like it would stand the test of time to mark the passage of the generations of Brandts who'd been born and raised there.

She'd looked online the night before while she'd taken a moment in the bathroom and read about the history of the family in Texas. It humbled her to see the many generations of Texans who'd called it home.

Standing in front of the house, she wondered what it would be like to have roots as solid as theirs.

Well, she'd wonder about that later. She had a job to do. She took a step forward, but before she could set foot on the porch, the front door opened, and Grayson Brandt stood there.

"You're Jemma's mom."

She nodded and swallowed the lump in her throat. "Yes."

"I'm pretty much an asshole these days. You sure you want to do this?"

"I'm here to cook and clean, Mister Brandt. That's all. If you think a sour attitude will change my mind, you would be wrong."

He stood there and looked her over.

Louise didn't have any misconceptions about that look. She had a feeling that he looked at horses and cows the same way.

"Well, you better come on in before I shut the door."

With an invitation like that, what could she do?

"Okay then." With a smile, she set the alarm on her car and headed for the door.

She had to stop when she was standing right in front of

Grayson. He was still standing in the doorway and didn't show any signs of moving.

Wondering what she'd missed, she looked up into his gaze and had to fight down the unfamiliar wave of heat that rose up inside of her.

"Something wrong, Mister Brandt?"

He lifted his chin toward her car in the drive. "No one here is going to take your things. You don't have to lock your car here."

Goodness.

Her cheeks heated and she felt like a complete nincompoop.

"I... I'm sorry, Mister Brandt. It's just a knee-jerk reaction. Where we were living, the cars up and down the street were always-"

"No need to explain. Just know that your things are safe here."

He moved away from the door, his cane alternating with his cowboy booted foot as he moved further into the house.

"Thank you," she said to his back. "I won't do it again."

He lifted a hand to brush away her assurance. "It's up to you, that's all I'm saying."

Yeah.

Okay.

As he continued through the living room, she followed behind him, wondering which foot was going to be the one she was going to stuff into her mouth.

She wasn't off to a good start, offending the boss within the first two or three minutes?

Priceless.

The main room was bigger than the small cottage she'd shared with Jemma. In fact, she could fit the backyard in there too.

That was easy enough to see as she walked around the furnishings.

And the hallway that she stepped into looked like it went on for a block.

Okay, she was probably exaggerating, but that's what it looked like from where she stood.

Housecleaning.

Louise blew out what she hoped was a silent breath as she mentally calculated what she needed to do.

"You can relax. I'm not expecting you to clean every inch of the place. Right now I just need to keep everything from being overrun with dust bunnies.

"I'd keep it clean on my own if I didn't have a metal rod in my leg."

She slowed and lowered her gaze to his injured leg, and she could see the contrast of the heavy fracture boot against his clothes more that she'd noticed before.

"I'm sorry you were hit."

He stopped short in the hallway, his back tense and stiff. "I don't need your *kind* words."

With the emphasis he'd put on that word, she had the feeling that he didn't need it because he was sorely lacking in that area himself at the moment.

But she wasn't about to say anything.

She'd seen Grayson teaching at the ranch's arena, and she'd seen his kindness to the children.

That was enough to tell her that his current... disposition wasn't the whole story.

He was in pain.

And she knew what it was like to be in pain. The thirty hours that she'd been in labor with Jemma had been enough to make her lose her temper. And Greg had been surly and downright mean close to the end of his life.

Pain, she could understand.

And pain wasn't going to get in the way of a job to help her raise her daughter.

"This," he almost grunted the word, "is your room."

"My room?" She turned her head to the side, canting her right ear toward him just in case she hadn't heard him quite right. "Jemma can sleep in there with me."

"Jemma can have the room at the end of the hall. You don't have to share. This house has half a dozen bedrooms."

Louise recoiled a little at that and she heard a gruff HA from Grayson.

"You don't have to clean them all. The ones that aren't used can be left as is."

She nodded, thankful for that revelation. "Okay. I see."

"There's a bathroom between the two bedrooms." He leaned against the wall and pointed his cane at the open doorway. "There."

"And your bedroom?"

He turned back toward her, and the look in his eyes made her run cold and hot at the same time. "Why do you need to know?"

She stammered as she leaned back and away from him. "No... no reason. Well, no, there is a reason." She had to calm her breathing and keep her gaze on his. "I can't clean your room unless I know where it is."

"You stay out of my room."

The pitch of his voice dropped down to where she almost didn't hear it, but there was no mistaking the foreboding look on his face.

"But I thought—"

"Don't think. Don't waste your time." He pushed away from the wall and moved down the hall past her and stopped at a door at the beginning of the hallway. "This, since you're so interested," he lifted his chin at the door before he pushed it in with his free hand, "is my bedroom. And I'm serious," his eyes narrowed on her face, "don't go inside. That's why I sent the last one packing."

He disappeared a moment later and the door slammed behind him.

"Okay," she breathed. "That went about as well as when Greg tried to teach me how to drive a stick."

She wondered if she'd make it longer than nightfall before he sent her, and Jemma, packing. Shaking her head, she left the house. She had hours and hours of work ahead of her to get them ready to move to the ranch the next day.

## CHAPTER FOUR

### Roped by the Dad Bod

Grayson leaned his forehead against the door and sighed.

"I'm an ass."

He hissed out the end of the word, sure that if Louise heard him, she'd gladly agree with him.

She'd shown up nice and early, and he'd been a total ass to her from word one.

Hell, she hadn't even come in the door, and he was already biting her head off.

He'd been grumbling and grouching at people since he'd come home from the hospital. It wasn't their fault that his rodeo career was over. He couldn't even summon much hate for the man who'd crashed into his truck.

He'd been driving exhausted, his eyes bleary and his head foggy. If he'd plowed into a smaller vehicle, the people in that car wouldn't have survived.

With the size of his truck, Grayson had survived the crash with what was on paper, a bad traffic accident, but the paper didn't come close to explaining what it had done to him beyond the physical results.

Grayson didn't want to drive anywhere. Not that he could with the cast before, nor with the fracture boot he had on now. He was basically captive on the ranch property.

Thanks to John, Grayson didn't even have to leave the house to go to the barn. All of that was taken care of by the hands who worked for them.

The whole thing grated on him.

Before the accident, he'd gone anywhere he liked. Walk to the barn, saddle up a horse, take off across Brandt land after chores were done.

He could see the sights that his ancestors had looked on with pride as sweat coursed over their skin. It was all there, stretched out before him, but now, it only seemed a reminder of what he'd been about to lose.

One moment between life and death and he'd come out somewhere in between. Locked away in a wooden box.

He didn't like the way it made him feel or the breathless way he struggled to put that all behind him.

He certainly didn't want people staying with him where they could see how much he was struggling.

Then why didn't he tell Louise to step off the way he'd done the others?

That was the million-dollar question, wasn't it?

It wasn't like he'd suddenly remembered his manners.

He'd always had those. His father had taught both of his sons the right way to behave from an early age.

But knowing how to behave and doing it were two different things, and he'd managed to chase off everyone else.

Not Louise, though.

Not that he'd put much effort into it.

There was something about her that... softened him in some ways.

He remembered her daughter Jenna from her riding lessons.

She was a natural. Better yet, Jemma listened to instructions. It was likely that her calm demeanor in the saddle is why she got along with them the way she did.

Horses liked settled, earthy people and Jemma was just that.

Now that he'd met her mother, he was pretty sure that she'd come by that part of her nature from her mother.

Solid, salt of the earth people.

Being in the same room with Louise had loosened some of the strain around his heart. Seeing the way she looked in his house and the nervous hesitation in her voice when he'd ordered her to stay out of his room made him feel...

Well, it made him feel like more of an ass.

Staring out the window at the empty driveway gave him a bit of heartburn. Lifting his hand, he pushed the heel of it against his chest and felt the emptiness inside.

He grumbled at himself as he limped to his armchair and settled himself in it and used his phone to turn on the radio.

He didn't turn on his television unless he was going to watch something like rodeo coverage. The rest of the offerings did little to entertain him.

Music, though... He liked music.

Cowboy songs, bluegrass bands, and some country found its way into his playlists, but that was about all that he could stomach.

Just as a classic Brooks and Dunn song came over the speakers, he heard bootfalls on his porch.

There wasn't time to stand up and lock the door before his brother strolled in.

"Hey, Gray." John shrugged out of his coat and set it on a

hook beside the door. "Looks like you're still alive. That's good to know."

When his brother dropped down onto the couch, leaned back, and stretched his arms across the back, Grayson shook his head.

"Go ahead, John. Come on in and have a seat."

His brother laughed out loud and tipped his head back. "I've lived here, too."

Grayson blew out a long breath and stretched his leg out, doing his best to ignore the twinge of pain he felt at the movement. "Is that why you're here now? You've ticked off your beautiful wife and she's finally come to her senses and kicked you out?"

John looked at him as if he'd kicked a puppy. "I came to see if you and Louise had gotten along. Now I'm wondering if she'll be back tomorrow after she got a taste of your moods."

Grayson slid a sidelong glance at this brother. "She's stronger than you give her credit for."

"Oh? So, she made an impression on you?"

"What are you getting at?"

John lifted his hands up in a vague gesture. "It's just a question, Gray." He shook his head. "Are you going to be this obnoxious when she moves in?"

Shifting on his chair, Grayson turned toward his brother and glared at him. "I know how to behave."

John's eyes widened a bit and his mouth dropped open.

"Shut up." Grayson reached for the cane that he'd leaned against the side table. "Don't make me beat you with this cane."

"Ha! You're feeling better. I can tell."

Grayson narrowed his eyes at his brother. "You should be glad I can't run after you yet."

John sobered a bit and leaned forward, bracing his forearms on his knees. "Seriously, Gray. I need you not to scare her away."

Grayson heard the somber tone of John's voice. It wasn't something he heard often. "What's going on?"

He could see John struggling with the answer.

"You don't have to tell me. I'm not planning on scaring her off. I don't have an interest in upsetting her. Especially with Jemma here. I'm an asshole, not a monster."

John's shoulders rose and fell as his lips pursed into a thin, colorless line. "Just promise me that you'll keep your temper in check. Louise and Jemma could use a few weeks in a welcoming home. Okay?"

Grayson shifted on the armchair again. "What's going on?"

For the first time in a long time, Grayson saw his brother look worried. Really and truly worried.

That's not to say that John didn't take things seriously. He had the same Brandt singular focus that had kept the family on top of the rodeo circuit for generations and made their ranch as big of a success as it had been.

"I should tell you... No. I think you should know..." He shook his head. "Have you ever wondered why you don't see Jemma's father around?"

"I hadn't thought about it." The words were true, but it didn't keep him from feeling a bit of an ass for not thinking about it. "What's going on?"

John swallowed and wrung his hands together. "He died, some kind of illness. I didn't ask for details, and really if you want to know more about that, you can ask Laney. I'm not the guy that Louise would tell all of that to. I just know from Laney that things are tough for Louise and her daughter. They need a place to collect themselves for a few weeks."

There were still pieces that Grayson didn't have. "The ranch is outside of town. Quite a bit. Will Louise be able to keep her job and he-" Grayson stopped when a pained look pulled at John's expression. "She lost her job?"

"Downsizing or restructuring... Something like that."

Something inside of Grayson twisted.

Hard.

"You could have said something before she came over."

John looked a little contrite at that. "I wanted to talk to you face to face but I ended up taking some time with Jemma after her lesson." He shrugged. "That's a crap answer, but I couldn't help it. She took a jump today!"

Grayson grinned at the news. "How was it?"

"She sailed Hawthorne right over the bar."

"Yeah?"

They were both wrapped up in the celebration for a moment. It wasn't hard to be distracted by Jemma. The girl was a natural and seeing her build up skills and confidence was exciting.

Still, his brother should have filled him in before Louise showed up at his house. "You get a pass... this time."

The slightly ominous warning wasn't lost on John, who laughed and held up his hands in surrender.

"I'm not joking, John. With her staying here at the ranch, can she get back to her own place when they leave?"

John hesitated for a moment. "They have to move soon anyway. Their landlord is selling their place. Staying here could be a huge help to her. If you have a problem with accepting help, could you just try to find a way to let her help around the house? Let her do something to help you. Laney and I are hoping you'll give her a chance to catch her breath."

Grayson leaned on the arm of his chair, and his mind

whirled with thoughts. Most of them weren't flattering. "I feel like an ass."

"I know you're a good guy, Grayson. You're the best older brother I could have asked for."

Grayson raised a brow at the comment, and John shrugged. "I know I haven't always appreciated having an older brother."

"We've certainly butted heads throughout the years, but we've always managed to stay family."

"Well, I've mellowed over the years," John added in.

"You're a dad now. A good one and a good husband."

"That means a lot coming from you, Gray." John swallowed hard, his Adam's apple working in his throat. "You know me better than most."

"And you know me, but you're worried that I'll scare Louise away."

"Can you blame me? You've been... a little off your feed since the accident."

His backbone stiffening, Grayson gave his brother a hard look. "You don't know what you're saying. Literally." Grayson chuckled a little and John blew out a breath and settled against the cushions for the first time. "But I get the stakes here, John. I'll be careful with her. With them."

"Okay." John got up and crossed over to his brother and gave him a good smack on the shoulder. "Thanks, old man. Glad we're on the same page."

John moved on to the door and stopped when he had the door open before him. "I got the idiom right this time."

Grayson nodded.

When John stepped out onto the porch, Grayson called out to him. "John!"

His brother spun around with a curious look on his face. "Hmm?"

"Your kids are lucky to have you as a father.."

"Yeah?" His smile brightened his face.

"Yeah," Grayson nodded. "You've got that dad joke thing down."

John rolled his eyes. "I'll see you in the morning, asshole."

Grayson nodded and John closed the door behind him.

## CHAPTER FIVE

## Roped by the DAD BOD

When Louise arrived the next morning, her daughter was still half asleep in the car. When they parked in the driveway of the ranch house, she had to nudge her awake so they could go inside. "Come on, sweet girl. I just need you to get up and go inside, you can sleep a little bit more while I make breakfast."

Breakfast was the word that roused Jemma. Her daughter's eyes fluttered open, and she yawned.

Even though Louise had been up for a few hours herself, she stifled her own yawn.

"Come on, Jemma. I bet it's warm inside."

"Mm-okay, Mama." Jemma swung her legs out of the open doorway and Louise couldn't ignore how cute her daughter looked in her cow printed PJs with her sock covered feet slipped into her hiking boots.

As Jemma walked past her, Louise pulled a wool beanie onto her daughter's head.

With that taken care of, she darted ahead and unlocked the door. Laney had assured her that she could just use the key, as there wasn't a security system in the old house.

She wouldn't have to worry about waking Grayson or having the police making a house call before she had the coffee going.

She opened the door just as Jemma stumbled through, her boots left behind on the mat. Her little girl found the couch face first and before Louise could cover her with a blanket, she was already fast asleep.

Louise smiled at the homey picture in front of her.

Jemma was a deep sleeper, like her father had been. Louise was an early riser who slept very lightly. A difference that hadn't been so bad until Jemma's dad passed away. Without that familiar buffer, Louise had to learn how to get her daughter up without a war starting in the household.

Leaving Jemma sleeping on the couch, Louise went outside and brought in the groceries that she'd picked up. It felt strange to add her purchases to the Brandt Ranch account at the grocery store in town, but the manager had called her by name and assured her that she wouldn't have a problem picking up supplies.

The one odd occurrence that happened at the end of her shopping trip that morning had been the strange looks from a couple of the older women who worked at the front of the store.

While she'd been unloading her cart onto the counter beside the cash register, she'd heard someone mention Grayson's name.

Louise hadn't turned her head to look, but there was a mirror-like shine to the light above the register and she'd lifted her gaze up enough to see the women talking and looking over at her with narrowed eyes.

Ah... small town speculation.

She hadn't had that happen much in her life. She'd been pretty unremarkable so far.

That was until she started buying groceries for the Brandt Ranch.

Now, she'd mused, she was a mystery woman.

A mystery woman buying lots of meat, eggs, cheese and vegetables.

Now, she was carrying them into the house from the car.

It was a mistake, she reasoned, as something in her back pinched on her third trip in from the trunk of her car. The idea had been to pick up enough for a couple of weeks, so she didn't have to leave much.

She didn't want Grayson to think she was trying to escape or something like that.

He'd already been a little cross with her when she'd gone to introduce herself, but she figured that he'd change his mind when he got used to her.

Either that or he'd tie her to a saddle and send the horse galloping away.

No, she shook her head, he wouldn't waste a horse like that.

The pantry and cabinets were easy enough to figure out. The person who'd set them up, or maintained them, had a really logical mindset.

The kitchen even had its junk drawer at the end of the counter, closest to the door. Just the place to drop odds and ends on the way out or in.

Perfect.

The things she'd decided not to purchase at the store she could still find in the kitchen and used some of the bread with the new eggs to prep some french toast while she got the bacon going along with the eggs.

She had planned to ask Grayson what he liked to eat the day before, but with their less than auspicious beginning, she didn't have the chance.

Today, she hoped that he liked what she made for breakfast and from there, she'd have a chance to move forward.

At least she knew that Jemma would be more than happy to dig into the breakfast she was making. The rest she'd figure out later.

She wondered if she should go and knock on Grayson's door, but she set aside that idea before she could seriously consider it. If he was asleep, the last thing she wanted to do was to surprise him by knocking on his door.

For a moment she smiled and thought about him as if he was a big grizzly bear sleeping in his cave during the winter.

The air certainly was chilly enough outside in the mornings to make the comparison possible. She could imagine him shuffling out of his room, his nose lifting in the air. The coffee pot sputtered and hissed, and she bit back a laugh, imagining the large bear leaning away from the machine, watching it wearily to see what else it would do.

Oh, her thoughts weren't mean or trying to paint Grayson in a bad light. She liked bears. As long as they were on the TV or in Facebook videos.

Bears had always fascinated her, even when her first experience with them was at Disneyland. The Country Bears Jamboree.

Louise sighed and shook her head. She'd read somewhere that it had been closed and she mourned its loss because she'd always meant to take Jemma to the amusement park and see her favorite bear, the one who blew over the mouth of a jar as his part in the band.

She hummed a tune as she turned one of the pieces of french toast over in the pan, tapping her feet as she turned the other piece over. The brown and gold of the toast made her smile.

She could almost taste it in her mouth.

Crispy, buttery deliciousness.

Louise hated to admit it, but she'd gotten out of the habit of cooking in the morning for breakfast. She'd never quite gotten the hang of waking Jemma up early enough that she could cook breakfast and get them both ready and out of the front door.

It wasn't that she hadn't had the time to get into the habit, she just hadn't managed it.

In all honesty, she'd almost given up, as things in her life were suddenly spiraling out of control.

She wasn't proud of the admission, but it was... what it was. Yet another failing.

The thought stole her breath, and she took a step away from the stove and leaned on the edge of the sink, closing her eyes before she started to cry.

What had led her to think that she could take care of Grayson Brandt when she couldn't even take care of her own life?

When Laney had suggested this job, she'd jumped at it.

She guessed that she could blame it on desperation, the same way that drowning swimmers grabbed onto anything thrown in their direction.

She dragged in a breath, hoping that it would be a boon to everyone involved, but suddenly she was wondering if she was going to pull Grayson down with her.

Louise shook herself, struggling to hold herself together.

With her momentary fascination with drowning, it was a good thing that the ranch wasn't near any large body of water.

From what she could see, the worst threat of drowning on the ranch was falling face first into a livestock trough.

Her job had nothing to do with those, so she was probably in luck.

Right?

A slight hissing sound turned her head and she saw the smoke coming up from the pan was a little darker than it should be.

Hissing a breath of her own, she picked up the spatula and lifted the two pieces of french toast out of the pan and set them on her plate.

She'd burned them, so she would eat them.

It was only fair, right?

## CHAPTER SIX

## Roped by the DAD BOD

Grayson woke up thinking he was dreaming. Bacon. He could smell bacon in the air. Bacon and coffee.

So seduced by the scents in the air, he almost fell out of bed onto his face. With his lower leg still wrapped in the fracture boot, it was difficult to bend it enough to get it under him.

He managed not to hit the floor and then had to maneuver himself so that he could reach his cane. With that in his hand, he moved to the back of his bedroom door and lifted his robe from the hook and shrugged it on.

The time it took to put on the robe and walk down the hall gave him time to piece his thoughts together. And to remind himself that Louise needed this job and he better not be a raving asshole, no matter what his natural state happened to be.

He paused at the end of the hall before he stepped into the main area of the house.

Grayson could hear Louise humming under her voice, but he wasn't sure what song it was.

Maybe it was the ringing in his ears that kept him from deciphering the tune.

It wasn't something he was used to, but it seemed to happen when he was deep in thought, as if his thoughts were too loud for him to hear the world at large.

He just wasn't used to having it happen in the house.

Standing there, watching a woman at his stove.

It wasn't something he'd say out loud or he might be accused of being a... a chauvinist. Or some other archaic kind of guy.

There was truth enough that he was an old-fashioned kind of guy, but he didn't expect a woman to do all of the housework.

He'd done things for himself when John and Laney moved to their own place on the ranch. He wasn't averse to the work at all, but breaking his leg had changed things for a time.

He'd moved in temporarily with his brother's family, but that only lasted so long. The moment he could get up and hobble around without his surgeon threatening to tie him down or sedate him, he moved back to his own place.

He just couldn't do as much for himself as he had before.

That's why he'd apparently terrorized a number of people that Laney had hired to care for him.

He was determined to do better.

Partly because of John's request, but also because he knew that Louise didn't deserve his stupidity. She had it hard enough.

"Dang it."

He frowned and leaned closer in her direction, wondering what had gone wrong.

Louise moved back to the stove from the sink and quickly

scooped up something from the pan on the stovetop and set them onto a plate.

Drawing in a deep breath through his nose, he scented the delicious smell of french toast. He hadn't had french toast for breakfast... or any other event for years and years.

The scent also told them that the two pieces had been burnt a little, but it didn't do a thing to make the smell any less tempting.

He didn't mind a few dark spots on food. He'd left more than enough on his food when he'd been the one doing most of the cooking in the house.

John, who'd lived with him for years, called them 'flavor spots.'

As two bachelors living with each other for years, they'd come up with many interesting ways to survive their less than expert skills at the stove and around the house.

The guys in the bunkhouse had better food than they did, but only because their skills were just passable.

The coffee pot sputtered again, and Louise moved to the side to grab up a potholder that he didn't recognize. She opened the door to the front of the stove and the scent of bacon suddenly drew in him.

"That smells amazing."

Louise jumped back and the cookie sheet in her hand clattered down onto the grate in the oven. "Oh, it's you."

"Sorry." He reached up a hand to scratch at the back of his neck. "I woke up to the smell of coffee and bacon and it's been so long since something that good was coming from this kitchen, I couldn't stay put in my room."

Louise was flustered.

The hand she had pressed to her chest was covering her heart and the other hand shook a little where it touched her cheek.

"You can go anywhere you want in the house, Mr. Brandt. I'm not complaining or upset, just a little... shocked. I was in my own thoughts a little too much." She shook her head as if she was trying to shake snow or a light rain from her hair. "Do you need help taking a seat at the table?"

He felt a muscle tick in his cheek, but just as soon as it happened, he moved his jaw, trying to help it relax.

"I'm fine."

Grayson wasn't sure that she'd even seen it. His beard sometimes hid some of his less than admirable expressions. It was one of the reasons why he'd left it there for the more than fifteen years that he'd kept it on his face.

Still, he dipped his chin down as he moved toward the kitchen table to take a seat. His instinct was for frustration to bubble up at the slightest provocation, but he was going to try to be better, or at least hide it as best he could.

"Thanks."

For her.

Grayson pulled out a chair and managed to sit down without falling into it.

That pleased him. The last thing he wanted was for Louise to think he was an invalid.

That thought surprised him.

Not that he'd want anyone to think he was weak, but the idea that he'd see something akin to pity on Louise's face rankled.

"I wasn't sure when you were going to be up, but I wanted to get here in time to cook something for breakfast."

"It smells good."

He caught her smile just as she turned to face the stove. The tray went down on the countertop, and she quickly took out a small stack of plates from the cabinet above the counter.

"I should have shown you around yesterday."

Louise turned halfway around and smiled at him before she turned back to do something at the counter. "That's very sweet of you to say, but I found everything easily this morning. You pretty much have everything in the cabinets in the way that I've arranged mine."

"Oh?"

He watched as she turned back to him at the table with a platter of sliced melon in one hand and the plates in the other.

Louise set the platter down first and then the plates in the center of the table.

After she set both down, she plucked a knife and fork from a basket on the table.

"I hope you don't mind, but I brought my silverware caddy here with me. If you don't like it, I can put it out in my car. It is a little kitschy, but it helps me keep things organized for the most part."

He reached out and picked it up by the top handle, which made it look a little like a picnic basket. "It looks handy."

He looked up at her and saw her smiling at him.

Something shifted inside of him, putting him a little off balance. He lowered the caddy and set it back on the table so he could brace his hand on the table.

That smile.

Her smile.

There was something about it, or about her, that settled inside of him and warmed him from the inside out.

To say it was unnerving was an understatement.

A smile.

He smiled a little at the absurdity of it all.

"How would you like your eggs?"

Her question cut through the strange haze of thoughts in his head, and he latched onto it like a life preserver tossed into the water.

"Anything is fine."

She dropped her chin a little and gave him a look that had him rethinking his vague reply.

"Over easy?"

She smiled again, deeper and broader this time.

The effect it had on him was even more than the first time. His cheeks warmed at the sight and his heart beat a little faster.

"I can do that." She turned back to the stove and tossed another comment over her shoulder. "See? That wasn't so hard, was it?"

He shook his head as though she could see him, but she couldn't.

Grayson knew he should say something, but he couldn't think of anything to say that wouldn't sound like he was an idiot.

It was at that moment that movement from the couch turned his head. Jemma sat up and the blanket that had been placed over her slipped down. "Hey, Mister Brandt!" She yawned, tipping her head back in a big, monster-sized stretch. "Did we wake you up?"

He gestured at the stove. "Breakfast did. Are you hungry?"

It was as if the word 'hungry' flipped a switch inside of Jemma.

Her nose lifted into the air, and she gasped, dropping her feet to the floor. "Is that pancakes?"

"Close." Jemma almost deflated as he watched, and Louise laughed softly. "I made some french toast, silly goose. Now go and wash up so you can eat breakfast."

Jemma dramatically dragged her feet across the floorboards for a few steps, making a fairly accurate imitation of a zombie shuffling away.

"You keep that up, young lady, and I'm going to eat these in front of you."

Jemma spun around, almost laughing. "Ha! You'd never do that!"

Grayson chuckled. "Are you sure, Jemma? Your mom looks like she's serious."

Jemma moved past her mother and reached for the sink to wash her hands.

Louise handed her daughter a paper towel to wipe her hands on when she was done. "It's true. It's just an empty threat. I don't use food as a punishment or reward."

Grayson sat back in his chair with her words echoing in his ears. "I never raised a child, but I can see what you're saying." His lips relaxed enough to smile. "Looks like I learned something new today and I didn't even have to leave my table!"

Louise and Jemma laughed with Louise's slightly deeper tone, making everything warmer. Jemma's easy laughter made him smile even more.

The muscles in his face protested the unfamiliar expression. Louise sat down in another chair at the table, and he found himself struggling not to watch her too closely.

Just the way she'd seemingly shrugged off their less than stellar meeting the day before made him respect her. She hadn't taken him to task for his rude behavior, although he knew he'd have to apologize soon, she wasn't pushing him to do what was right.

She wasn't a shrinking violet in the least. She seemed to have a steel spine and while he knew he was a mess and rumpled after a hard night of sleep, she looked wide-awake and fresh.

He hadn't done her any favors and sadly, he might have cheated himself out of this unexpected domestic moment.

And by the smell of those pieces of french toast, a tasty meal.

Louise placed a platter of french toast on the table and a bottle of maple syrup that made his mouth water just by looking at it.

Before he could reach for anything, Louise followed it with a platter of bacon that was cooked to perfection. "How did you know?"

Her brows raised. "Know what?"

"How I like my bacon." He gestured at the plate. "That's a beautiful thing you have there."

"Ah." Louise turned and brought the coffeepot over to the table and set it on a trivet. "Well, is there any other way to make bacon?" She smiled and he found himself smiling with her.

"I know, mom."

Grayson turned to look at Jemma, who was perched on her chair with big eyes and a bigger grin. "What's that?"

Jemma tipped her face down a little and Grayson wondered if he'd been too loud.

"Go ahead." He put his hand on the tabletop. "Tell us."

Jemma looked over at her mom first. Grayson saw Louise nod at her daughter.

"It's just that mom puts bacon on our turkey for Thanksgiving. It doesn't get crispy or anything like that, but it's still super tasty."

Grayson agreed. "Bacon on a turkey. That sounds like the best thing to put on a bird."

Happy that Jemma hadn't stayed bashful for long, he reached out and picked up a pair of pinchers and went after a few pieces of bacon. When he held the crispy strips above Jemma's plate, he looked over at Louise and saw her looking back at him with a soft expression. "How much should I put on her plate?"

"That's fine. Thank you."

Grayson saw the careful way that Louise was watching him. He wondered what it would be like if she was comfortable with him. Would her choice of words change? Or her tone?

A mixture of both?

He put the bacon strips on the plate and saw the hungry gleam in Jemma's eyes, he completely agreed with her. "You want some french toast?"

"Of course!" Jemma leaned a little closer. "My mom's french toast is the best. It's crispy and she puts cinnamon in the egg."

"Cinnamon, huh?"

Jemma nodded, her lopsided pig tails shaking loose. "It's suuuuper good."

"Super, huh?"

Grayson turned back to serve the french toast and already saw a few pieces on his plate.

Louise gave him a knowing grin as she reached out and put a couple of pieces on her daughter's plate. "I think you'll like it." She took a piece for her own and set the pinchers on the platter as she reached for the bottle of maple syrup and stood. "I've never had any complaints."

She drizzled the syrup over Jemma's toast and leaned in to place a kiss on the crown of her daughter's head. "Remember to use your napkin."

Jemma's fork was already cutting into the pieces of toast. "Sure, mom."

Grayson already had a piece of the french toast in his mouth without syrup. He saw Louise's curious stare and managed to put on a little smile with his lips held closed.

She put syrup on the rest of his toast as he swallowed the bite he had in his mouth.

"It's good. Really good."

Louise smiled, her cheeks pinking with a blush. "I'm glad you think so."

Oh, he did, and as he took a bite of the toast with syrup, he realized that things were so much better than good.

He was really warming up to the idea of having the both of them around.

## CHAPTER SEVEN

### Roped by the Dad Bod

Things were going well.

Almost too well.

At least, that's what her inside voice was telling her.

Her meeting with Grayson the day before had left her a little hesitant about working for him, but if it wasn't for her current situation, she might have been tempted to look for another job.

But realistically, what job came with a place to live? And that place to live? That meant everything. It meant she could have her daughter somewhere safe.

She knew that Jemma loved the ranch. When she was taking lessons on Saturdays, she talked about the ranch every afternoon when she got home from school. And right before bed at night.

It was going to be something special for Jemma to be on the property for a few months during the summer.

John sent a hand to collect Jemma after breakfast. He'd brought over one of the horses she'd ridden in her lessons and

Jemma had swung herself up in the saddle to go to the barn and help curry the horses.

Jemma had explained to her that it meant she'd help groom the horses and give them some of their feed.

She'd held back a comment about how difficult it was to get Jemma to pick up her things around her bed. It wasn't the time to bring it up. Not in front of a ranch hand and Grayson.

Whatever they wanted her to do at the barn, Jemma was excited to do it.

What a change.

That gave Louise a chance to familiarize herself with the house and start her chores.

Her cell phone rang, and she pulled it out of her pocket and managed to flip it open using one hand so she could still wipe the shelf in the refrigerator.

"Hello?"

"Louise, hi! This is Laney!"

"Laney, hello. What's going on?"

Laney's laughter was light and easy. "You sound like you're elbow-deep in something serious."

Louise drew back and looked out the kitchen windows. "Are you outside and watching me?"

"Oh? I was that close, hmm?"

Louise continued to scrub the shelf, unwilling to leave the door open longer than she needed to. "I'm cleaning the refrigerator. Looking to see what kinds of supplies I'll need to cook."

"You got right down to business! I bet... You know, I have no idea how Gray is taking it."

"Everything's great." Louise meant it. So far, so good. Breakfast had been fun. Surprisingly so. "I just wanted to get a good look at what I need to pick up. I'm not all that eager to take the drive into town often."

"Oh, I know. It's a bit of a trip to make."

Louise tucked the phone between her ear and her shoulder so she could move around some of the bottles in the back of the refrigerator.

"Yeah. I picked up a bunch of things this morning at the store. I got a few strange looks from other customers when the manager said he'd put it on the ranch account. I hope I'm not making things weird for any of you."

"From the customers, huh?" Laney's voice was a little hesitant and soft. "Women customers?"

It took Louise a moment to think about it while she drew a bottle of pickles to the front that looked like they'd been hidden back there for a good long time.

"You know, I think they were."

"Ah..." Laney giggled. "I got some of the same looks when John took me down to add me to the ranch account. Apparently, the town was wondering when the Brandt boys would settle down. They kept their eyes on me when I first saddled up with the family. Now they probably think you're moving in with Grayson."

"But I am... I mean, I did move in with Grayson- Oh. Like that. Oh, I guess I should have clarified that I'm the housekeeper."

"Don't worry about it," Laney laughed a little more, "they'll think whatever they want no matter what. You could have produced a written employment letter and they'd just come up with something in their heads and go with it."

"I've always heard it was like that in a small town, but I didn't think I'd end up in this situation."

"What kind of situation is that?"

"Uh..." Louise tensed up a little in her back. "Laney? Mister Brandt-"

"Call me Grayson, Louise."

She closed her eyes and winced. "Grayson's here. I'll talk to you later."

Laney's laughter deepened into chuckles. "Don't let him grump at you. He's just a big ol' teddy bear."

Louise managed not to burst out laughing. "Okay. I'm going to go. Bye."

She pulled out the bottle of pickles as she folded her phone closed and dropped it into her jeans pocket.

Louise closed the refrigerator door and met his gaze with her own, determined not to be cowed by his mood, no matter what.

"Can I help you with something, Mister- I mean, can I help you with something, Grayson?"

Saying his name to him gave her a little thrill. A little shiver ran down her spine.

When Jemma had taken lessons from him, he'd been Mister Brandt, but Louise had slipped when she was talking to Laney and called him by his first name.

Now, it was really old-fashioned to hesitate calling him by his name, but she was working for the man and not just getting to know him. That's why she had meant to call him by the more... removed version of his name, but she'd made the blunder of calling him by his first name on the phone.

She was worried that he'd told her to call him by his first name because she'd already done it, not because he wanted her to.

And yes, even though he'd been nice that morning, she really didn't want to mess anything up. Not so soon after the start.

He was just looking at her, which was a bit unnerving.

"I'm sorry," she breathed. "I didn't mean to call you Grayson, but I was on the phone-"

"With Laney," he interjected. "And that makes sense. Laney never had a problem calling me Grayson. Or Gray."

She smiled, but she knew it was hesitant and probably a little brittle.

Nerves. She chalked it up to nerves.

Not because he'd gotten dressed and was wearing a dark burgundy shirt that made her fingers itch to touch it. It looked so soft and warm.

"I never expected you to call me Mister anything."

Her shoulders rose a little. "I guess because I'm working here, I felt like I should be more formal."

He smiled, and her eyes widened.

"What?"

"We don't really do formal around here, unless you count bolo ties and our good cowboy boots. Maybe even a shirt with snap buttons made out of mother-of-pearl."

She was left staring at him. "Really?"

"Well, fancy dressing is more John's thing. I like a pair of comfortable boots, a clean flannel shirt, and some jeans."

Louise couldn't help smiling at him, an expression she wasn't sure how much she'd use after being on the receiving end of his surly behavior.

"'That sounds about right."

"So you go ahead and call me Mister Brandt if you want. Or you can call me Grayson. Whatever makes you more comfortable."

He was being... almost too easy to talk to. She didn't think he was a complete jerk, but she certainly hadn't expected this kind of change in his demeanor overnight.

She was somehow tempted to ask him if he'd been visited by three ghosts the night before.

Tempted, but that didn't mean that she was going to needle him like that.

She'd just be happy that he was in a good mood and leave it there.

Now wasn't the time to push for anything.

Louise was still incredibly grateful for the opportunity to work and live on the ranch. The last thing she was going to do was threaten it by speaking out of turn.

"Okay." She nodded her head. "I'll think about and see which one I feel comfortable with."

Nodding, he looked down at the floor, tapping his cane on the hardwood. "Okay. I'm going to go and put my leg up for a bit."

She watched him turn away, and while she was trying to keep things on an even keel, she couldn't help herself from calling out to him.

"Grayson?"

His feet stopped and he turned slowly until he could see her over his shoulder. "Yeah?"

She wanted to hide her face in her hands, but she was too old- too mature for that kind of silliness.

"Are you sure I can't help you?"

Something crossed his face, like a shadow or a dark emotion. "I don't need it. I just... don't."

Her heart squeezed tight in her chest as his words brought back older, more painful memories than she'd ever admit.

"Okay." She licked at her lips, needing the familiar movement to ease the tension in her body. "Sorry. I know what you said before."

Grayson turned so all she could see was his back. It wasn't meant to be rude. At least she didn't think so.

He moved further away from her, and she turned away from him, too.

Blowing out a silent breath, she worried that she'd taken

the progress that they'd made and tossed it in the compost heap.

*Why?*

Well, that was the problem.

She didn't know.

# CHAPTER EIGHT

## Roped by the Dad Bod

A week later, Grayson found himself in his bathroom before breakfast. It wasn't just about washing his hands. He was trimming his beard.

Nothing drastic, just making sure that everything was... in line. Cleaning up any scraggly bits.

And he didn't just throw on a robe over his sleep shirt, he'd wrapped up his leg and fracture boot and sat on the shower chair to scrub himself clean to within an inch of his life before dressing and joining the rest of his...

He stopped in his doorway and listened to the easy banter in the main room.

He was just about to say family.

He chuckled silently.

Family.

Maybe if he hadn't had his head focused on the ranch for his entire adult life, he would have a family.

But Louise and Jemma weren't his.

And if things went to Laney's plan, they'd be moving on at the end of summer. He'd be back to roaming around the house by himself and Louise and her daughter would be back in town during the week with Jemma coming for lessons on the weekend.

His throat tightened at the thought.

Grayson had originally cringed at the thought of two people walking by his bedroom door again and again.

He was used to quiet in the house.

Quiet suited him.

That, and it wasn't a problem if he got up in the middle of the night and went to the kitchen half-naked.

Well hell, he could walk to the kitchen stark naked if he wanted to.

Grayson shook his head with a rueful smile on his lips. When was the last time he'd gone even half-naked around the house when he was alone?

Never.

He sighed at his own ridiculousness and heard the conversation in the main room come to a halt.

"Grayson?"

Hearing Louise call out his name from the other room had a few unexpected reactions.

First, he liked the way his name sounded in her voice.

She'd been hesitant to call him by his first name at the beginning, but once he'd encouraged her to do it, it had quickly become the norm.

And that brought up his second problem.

How *much* he liked hearing it.

It gave him a certain amount of satisfaction that she hadn't been cowed by him. That it took a day or two for her to stop lowering her voice to nearly a whisper when she said it made him feel relieved.

He was an ass, but he didn't want her to worry about being in his house. This time for her and for Jemma was too important.

He planted his cane and stepped out into the room. "I hope I'm not interrupting."

Jemma jumped up from her chair and pulled his chair out and away from the table. "I've got your chair for you."

Grayson's cheeks heated up with an uncomfortable flush. "I uh..." He looked up and saw Louise watching him. She didn't look worried. She looked... amused.

He smiled at her and then looked down at Jemma. Louise's sweet daughter beamed up at him. "Don't worry, I won't let you fall!"

He shook his head. "I wasn't worried about that, Jem. You're a good girl."

Her eyes blinked in surprise. "Cool! Hey, Mom!"

Grayson leaned back to try and escape the unexpectedly loud boom of Jemma's voice.

Louise looked like she was holding back laughter. "Yes, sweetie? I think the horses heard you at the barn."

"Oops!" Jemma covered her mouth with one hand. "Sorry," her voice was noticeably softer, "I get loud when I'm excited."

He moved between the chair and the table and sat down when he felt the chair touch the backs of his legs. "Thanks, Jem."

She sat down beside him and lifted a platter for him. "I like that. Jem."

He picked up a few of the pancakes and set them on his plate. "I like it, too."

"Mom?" Jemma turned to her mom. "What about you?"

"Jem's a great name," she nodded. "It reminds me of a book I read before."

That brightened the smile in Jemma's eyes. "Oh, yeah?" She turned toward him. "What about you, Mister Brandt? Did you read that book too?"

He looked across the table at Louise. "Mockingbird?"

She smiled. "The very same."

Jemma touched his arm. "Was Jem a cool girl in the book?"

He grimaced a little. "Well, Jem was a boy in the book."

"A boy?" Jemma sat back in her chair, a little pout on her lips.

"Why don't we see if we can get the book at the library and read it," Louise suggested. "Maybe you'll like the name in spite of it belonging to a boy."

Jemma thought through her mother's words before she nodded. "Okay. I can do that. When can we go to the library?"

"I have the book in my office, I think." Grayson liked the smile on both of their faces. "I think I have all of my books from my school years in there. I'm a big reader. Always have been."

Jemma brightened again. "Me and Mom, too! That's so cool!"

"Yes," Louise poured him a coffee and one for herself. "Yes. It's super cool."

She went back to cutting up her pancake, but Grayson wasn't ready to dive in just yet.

"You said you get loud when you're excited."

"Huh?" Jemma paused with her fork up in front of her mouth. "Oh, yeah."

She put the big bite of food in her mouth.

"I do."

Grayson looked over at Louise seated on the other side of the table and noticed that she was hiding her smile behind her glass of orange juice.

Jemma swallowed it down a few seconds later and Grayson worried that she might end up choking on her next bite.

"I was just wondering why you don't get loud at the arena."

Jemma lowered her fork to her plate and tilted her head to the side. He swore he could see the gears turning in her head.

When her head tipped back into its normal upright position, he imagined a light bulb over her head flaring to life.

"It's something my mom said."

Grayson turned to look at Louise, but she was looking at her daughter, her brow furrowed over the bridge of her nose.

He'd thought to ask Louise what she'd said to her daughter, but given the look on her face, she didn't remember it at the moment.

Instead, he turned back to look at Jemma. "What did your mom say?"

Jemma let go of her fork and cupped both of her hands around her mouth after she turned toward his seat. "My mom," she was whispering, but he could clearly hear her words, "said that horses are like sweet babies. We should be quiet and calm around them."

"Sweet babies." He repeated the words and turned to Louise. "I've never heard it said that way before."

Louise's cheeks were pink with a blush, and he had to flatten his hands on the tabletop to keep himself from reaching out across the table to touch her cheek and see if it was as warm as it looked.

"Why would you say it like that?"

She hesitated, her teeth biting into the corner of her lower lip.

"What you said was right," he tried to reassure her. "It's just I've never heard it said just like that."

Louise's hand raised to her cheeks, covering them as if she didn't like the heat in her skin. "It's something I thought of when we were driving here for her first lesson. I had one lesson when I was her age."

Grayson saw Jemma lean forward against the edge of the table, watching her mother with open curiosity.

"Why one, Mom?"

"It was supposed to be more, but Grandma Irene said her heart couldn't take it."

"What did Grandma have to do with it?"

"It's nothing, really."

Grayson set his fork down and leaned forward a bit on his own, too. "I'd like to know, if that's all right."

Louise's face paled a little and he regretted that he'd encouraged her to tell the story.

"You don't have to," he added. "I was just curious."

"Me, too!" Jemma winced and lowered her voice again. "It's hard to think that grandma took you to lessons. She didn't like animals. She didn't even want me to get a hamster."

Louise nodded and her expression softened.

"She didn't like animals. You're right. She hated them in all sizes, but my father promised me riding lessons, but he was working that day. So, grandma took me to the stables. She must have crossed herself a dozen times before I even got up in the saddle.

"The young woman giving the lessons was very sweet and tried to help grandma relax."

Jemma laughed and promptly hid her smile behind both of her hands. "Yeah, right."

"I think there were just three or four of us there for the introductory lesson, and-"

"What's introductory?"

Louise smiled at her daughter. "It means the first of many. At least," she looked at Grayson and he froze, "that's what I'd say without a dictionary."

Jemma turned to look at him. "Cool, right?"

He grinned back at her. "Cool?"

Jemma shrugged. "I've been watching old TV shows from the 80s. Everything was cool back then."

"Ah." He found himself smiling enough that the corners of his eyes were pressing together. "Well, if you want, we can go find the dictionary in my office after breakfast and you could look up the word."

"Cool!" Jemma picked up her fork for another bite of the pancake. Just a heartbeat shy of her mouth, she turned back to Louise. "So what happened with grandma?"

Grayson swore he saw Louise grimace. Maybe she was hoping they wouldn't get back to the story.

He was glad she was wrong.

"We all got up on the horses using the rails as a step to get up into the saddle. The next step was just getting the horses to walk around the arena.

"Easy. Nothing more strenuous than that. We weren't up in the saddle for more than twenty minutes or so, because we were going to get back off and head to the barn to learn how to groom the horses. I was the last one still in the saddle, waiting for the teacher to come around and show me how to get down.

"A car drove by the barn, sending up a huge cloud of dust. Just as they were about to drive out of sight, someone in the car shouted and then the others joined in. The sound spooked the horse, and she took off."

Grayson's stomach twisted in his gut. He'd seen the same thing happen a time or two in other places. He'd seen children with worse injuries than his after a horse had been spooked.

"Wow," Jemma stared wide-eyed at her mother. "What happened then?"

Louise's shoulders lifted just before her lips. Smiling, she looked at her daughter and shook her head. "I couldn't tell you much about it. I think I was in a kind of panic at the time.

"All I really remember was that if my mother, grandma, hadn't fainted, I might still be riding that horse into the sunset.

"The stable owner got a hold of the horse's reins and stopped it. He said that after the people in the car yelled my mother started to yell. He was surprised and said he was pretty impressed that I didn't let go of the reins."

"I'm impressed that you held on."

Grayson didn't realize that he had been the one who spoke until Louise looked at him, a sheepish grin on her lips.

"Really?"

He shrugged and nodded. "Yeah. A runaway horse? Your first lesson! You could have been ki-"

"Hurt," she finished for him, her eyes begging him not to say what he'd been about to. "I could have been, but I wasn't."

"How, mom?" Jemma didn't miss a beat.

"How...?"

"How did you stay in the saddle?"

Louise hesitated. Her skin seemed almost green for a moment.

Jemma turned her big eyes to Grayson and he reached out a hand, setting it on her shoulder. He didn't want her to be afraid. "Maybe we should leave this story until later."

Jemma turned back to her mom. "Why, mom? Everything turned out okay, right?"

Louise nodded and managed a smile.

He knew it was probably crazy, but for a moment he thought that maybe her smile was for him, too.

"Everything turned out fine." She agreed.

"Okay." Jemma nodded and the gesture was like an exclamation point, putting an end to the pause. "So what happened?"

Grayson was sure he saw a look of resignation on Louise's face.

"Well, once they got my mom calm enough not to start shouting and scaring the horses again, the man who owned the stables sat me down on a picnic bench or something like it, and he asked me how I managed to stay in the saddle and not fall off when the horse started to run."

Grayson relaxed when he saw Louise's smile almost turn into a laugh.

"I gave him a look, barely managing to keep myself from passing out from relief and told him. 'I held on because I didn't know there was another option?'"

Grayson felt the knot in his gut release itself. "Thank God you held on! That could have been-"

"But it wasn't." She gave him a subtle nod and then she darted a glance at her daughter, who was grinning as she chewed her pancakes. "That's why when Jemma asked to take lessons, I looked for the best place and found Brandt Ranch. I knew that she'd get the best instruction here." She turned a thoughtful look out through the window in the side door. "I think that's why I told Jemma about being quiet around horses. I don't really think about that moment in my life very often."

"I don't blame you." He let the conversation die there to give Louise a chance to relax. He understood why she'd been a little reticent about telling it in front of Jemma.

He didn't have to worry about filling the quiet as Jemma jumped in with a new topic a moment later.

Grayson was really beginning to enjoy the not-so-quiet around the house.

## CHAPTER NINE

## Roped by the DAD BOD

Louise was seated in a chair a little later, reading a book that she'd brought with her to the ranch. Absorbed in the words and the world written on the pages, she didn't hear Grayson walk into the room until he spoke up standing right behind her.

"That must be a great book."

She gasped in a breath, almost jumping up from her chair.

"Sorry. I'm sorry, Louise." Grayson took a step to the side, putting some space between them, and Louise couldn't help the strange feeling that came over her. She felt a little colder with him stepping away. "I didn't mean to frighten you."

She slipped her pointer finger between the pages to hold her place as she settled into the chair again. "You didn't really frighten me," she explained, "just a little shock. I didn't hear you come in."

His own eyes widened as he sat down in the armchair beside the sofa. "Then you must have been really involved in the book and I'm even more sorry. I know what it's like to be completely in a book and get yanked out of it."

His tone was softer than it had been on the first day when she'd come to his house. His expression had softened as well.

She didn't make a big deal about it thinking that he might not like the obvious stated. Instead, she looked at him, smiling. "Do you need anything? Hungry? Thirsty?"

"No. No, thanks. I just wanted to come out here and see what you're up to."

"I've done all of the daily chores." She winced after blurting out the words. "Sorry. I didn't mean to hurl the words at you."

"And I didn't feel like they were hurled."

They smiled at each other, falling into an easy quiet.

Louise looked at the clock on the wall. Laney had come by after breakfast to take Jemma to the barn and it was likely one of the ranch hands or John who would bring her daughter back for dinner.

Dinner.

She turned slightly and saw that Grayson was sitting quietly in the armchair, his head tipped back, his eyes closed and as she watched, his chest rose and fell with each breath.

Goodness. It was her first chance to just look at him.

They'd been there for just about a week, but that's how long it had taken to get caught up with the chores and cleaning around the house.

At first, Grayson had told her over and over again that she didn't have to clean the whole place.

But, again and again, she'd just cleaned things.

It wasn't that she was all that eager to do it, but she didn't want to sit around and even worse than that. She didn't want him to think she was just twiddling her thumbs.

After a full week of cleaning, she could run her fingers over any surface and not pick up dust.

It felt good.

It felt...

Like home.

The unbidden and uneasy thought stole her breath.

She didn't have a home.

Not one of her own.

This place and this situation were for the summer.

A few months of peace and quiet, saving money to start over with her daughter. The first real new beginning since...

Louise got up from the couch as quietly as she could, smiling to herself when Grayson didn't move a muscle.

He must be asleep.

Louise opened her book and set it down where she'd been sitting, open and face down on the cushion. She was careful not to crack the spine, but she didn't have a bookmark with her.

Leaving it there, she moved to the other end of the couch and picked up a blanket that she'd freshly washed.

Grayson had told her she could leave it alone, but she'd waited until he'd gone into his room to add it to the laundry. Now, she moved a little closer to him, carefully watching his face to see if he'd wake up.

But he didn't.

Instead, he breathed in and out in easy intervals.

When she was standing by the armchair, she took a moment to look her fill.

Grayson Brandt was a handsome man. Tall, and big all over, he reminded her of Grizzly Adams or Ron Pearlman in Magnificent Seven. Yes, she did have a thing for guys in the Old West or on the Frontier. Big, vibrant men who looked like they could pull a wagon if the horses needed a break.

She rolled her eyes at her wistful thoughts, blinking back a sudden onslaught of stinging tears.

Grayson wasn't anything like...

No, she wasn't going to compare the two that way. She wasn't going to put their names side by side.

Her husband had been in her life for so many years and they'd been such a good team alone and as parents.

They'd seen each other through problems and troubles, always standing beside each other.

When she'd lost him, she might have just curled up and cried herself into oblivion, but she had Jemma. And Jemma needed her more than she needed herself.

That's how she kept going.

And now, Jemma was thriving.

Laney and John were texting her photos of her little girl looking like a real cowgirl and doing some jumps on one of the horses.

It was like seeing a sunflower open and turn to the sun.

Jemma was blossoming just like that.

And herself?

Louise shook her head.

She was standing there, watching a man sleep.

A man who was too handsome for her own good.

It was easier, she realized, when he'd been a jerk and rude. When he was a bear to deal with, she knew she could do the job and keep herself separate from Scrooge Brandt.

Now?

He'd given her daughter a nickname, one that Louise was sure would stick.

He'd even gone into his office and brought out an old, dog-eared copy of *To Kill a Mockingbird*.

Grayson had brought it into the kitchen after Jemma left for the barn and he'd asked if it would be okay to lend it to her daughter.

Being a booklover herself, Louise had barely been able to keep herself from tearing up over the offer.

And now she was hoping that they'd find more that they shared in what they liked.

Not that she wanted a deeper connection with him. She just wanted to make their time together easier on all of them.

Leaning over Grayson, she draped the blanket over him. The well-worn blanket went from his chest, all the way down to over his knees.

She carefully avoided touching his leg for fear that she'd cause him pain and wake him up.

Still, he kept breathing slowly and deeply as she took a few stolen moments to watch over him.

Crazy as it seemed, the grumpy gus at the head of the house seemed to be softening a bit. And what she saw, she liked.

A lot.

He hummed in his sleep before mumbling something under his breath.

Louise squinted a little as she canted her head to the side, listening in.

He said something else, but she couldn't quite hear enough vowels or consonants to make out the words.

Worried that putting the blanket over him had been a mistake, she leaned in even closer so she might hear his words.

But he didn't speak again.

Worried more about his comfort rather than anything else, Louise opened her mouth.

"Grayson? I-"

He came awake with a soft, indrawn gasp and his hand took hold of her arm, just above her elbow. "Lou?"

He might have said her whole name, but the second half was lost in a bit of a sleepy slur of sound.

"What... what's going on?"

To say she was startled was an understatement.

His hand on her arm didn't hurt. His fingers didn't bite into her skin or pinch.

No, Grayson's hand on her arm was warm.

Warm and heavy, but not in a bad way.

Heavy like when a man leaned over her in bed, covering her body with-

"Are you okay, Louise?"

She managed a smile even though her face was red with heat. "Me? Oh... I'm good."

Louise tried to move back, but his hold on her arm didn't allow for her to put any more distance between them.

"You need somethin'?"

His voice was thick, his eyes heavily lidded.

And if her mind was working, he'd just looked at her lips.

Oh god.

"Lou?"

She breathed in, struggling to keep her heart from pounding in her chest. It wasn't easy because the weight of his hand was drawing her closer.

The only thing keeping her focused was the knowledge that she couldn't lean into him because she'd hurt his leg.

The last thing she wanted to do was cause him pain.

"I just put a blanket on you. You looked cold."

His eyes opened a little wider and she felt the weight of his gaze on her face. "I'm not cold."

"Because," she measured out her words, "you have a blanket now."

Grayson's chin tipped down and he looked at his chest and legs. "Oh."

He let go of her arm and she backed up, lifting her right hand to warm the spot where he'd just uncovered her skin.

Louise knew her hand wasn't enough to fill the emptiness.

That realization drove her back another couple of steps.

She'd taken things too far, which was strange enough. It had been a while since a simple touch had done so much to stir up her... emotions?

Chemistry?

Both?

"Louise?"

She swallowed hard at the knot in her throat. "I... I need to go and... I need to-"

Her mind was a mess.

Her heart pounding and stuttering in her chest.

It was chemistry, she reasoned.

That's what it had to be.

It wasn't emotional. No. That...

It couldn't be that.

It was pure chemistry.

A spark.

Lightning in a bottle.

And she couldn't allow it to flash over.

She was there, in Grayson's house, to take care of it.

To take care of him.

It wasn't the same as playing house.

That was something she'd had once. Something real.

This... wasn't.

This was heat. Chemistry. A yearning that just proved that she was alive.

Yes.

That's all.

That's all it was.

That's all it was going to be.

"I need to take care of some things."

Before the last word had cleared her lips, she was on the move, heading into the hall and into her temporary bedroom.

It wasn't until she fell face first onto the bed, grabbing up a pillow in her hands, that she felt like she could get a hold of her feelings.

Wrapping her arms around the pillow, she pulled it to her chest and hugged it tight. Tight enough to work an ache into her muscles.

And that helped her to focus again.

It helped to remind her who and what she was in this house.

She was the housekeeper.

She wasn't his.

And he, sadly, wasn't hers.

## CHAPTER TEN

## Roped by the DAD BOD

A week later, Louise was beginning to feel a little anxious.

A little trapped.

It wasn't anything that Grayson was doing on purpose. She was sure of that.

He was just doing what came naturally to him, and that's what was upsetting her.

Grayson had lent Jemma his copy of To Kill a Mockingbird, but instead of just putting it in her hands, he'd been there, encouraging her to read it.

When there was a difficult word, he'd helped her daughter tackle it as much as she had.

Together, they'd developed into a bit of a team and instead of wanting to turn on the TV that streamed shows over Wi-Fi, Jemma could sit on the sofa and read aloud with Grayson beside her in case she needed a hand.

Louise spent the time that she wasn't needed to answer a question, tucked into Grayson's armchair with a skein of yarn, working stitches for a plain afghan that she vaguely remembered from her childhood.

It was all too perfect for her heart to handle.

Her daughter wasn't just biding her time during the summer months, she was thriving.

Her eyes were bright, and it felt like her smile had doubled in size, stretching from ear to ear.

"Why does everyone make up stories about Boo?" Jemma was tucked up against Grayson's side, looking up at his face.

Louise watched carefully, too, wondering what he was about to say.

"I think that sometimes people see what they want to see and believe what they want to believe."

Jemma's brow furrowed above her nose. "But no one sees Boo. So what is it that they think they see?"

"Hmm..." Grayson paused, his gaze lifting up toward the rafters.

Beside him, Jemma seemed to copy his thoughtful post.

"I think a lot of people see their own fears in other people. It's easier to deal with things if you look at it from outside of the problem. When you're inside, it's all around you. It's hard to... catch your breath without choking on it."

Louise's hands paused. Her fingers lost their sure hold on the crochet hook and the little metal tool slipped from her fingers and fell between her thigh and the arm of the armchair.

She wanted to dig her hand into the space and fish it out, but she felt like she might startle Grayson or Jemma and the last thing she wanted to do was break the spell that they all seemed to be under.

"I've felt like that."

Louise froze then, her breath locked in her chest as she listened.

"Yeah?" Grayson leaned in an inch or two toward Jemma,

but his focus was listening. It was easily seen on his face and she felt it in her heart.

He was really sweet with Jemma and that went deep into her soul. Not just as a mother, but as a woman.

Jemma nodded, but she lowered her gaze and leaned against his shoulder. "People at school were really nice when my dad died. Everyone came up to tell me how sorry they were. It almost felt like... like I was the one making them feel better.

"I don't think they knew how tired I was every day. People just kept telling me how sorry they were for me. And I... I felt like it was happening over and over."

Louise was stunned at her daughter's words, but what cut down to her soul was the way that Grayson pulled Jemma into a hug, holding her tight as she began to cry.

Dropping the yarn that she'd held in her hands, Louise pushed herself out of the armchair and moved over to the sofa.

She carefully sat down next to Jemma, and it wasn't more than a moment or two before Grayson noticed she was there and turned Jemma around toward her.

Louise pulled her daughter into her embrace, murmuring soothing words to Jemma as her little girl tucked herself into a little ball and squeezed her arms around Louise's neck.

"Oh, sweetheart. I had no idea."

Jemma nodded against her neck and Louise felt Jemma's hand start to pat her against her back.

It was the same thing, Louise realized. Her daughter trying to comfort her instead of accepting the comfort for her.

"I'm okay, sweetie. You don't need to take care of me. I can take care of you. Okay?"

Jemma leaned back, lifting her face so that they could look into each other's eyes. Sniffling, Jemma gave her a watery smile. "I know. I know, mom. You're always there for me, but I can be there for you, too. We both lost daddy."

Tears flowed freely for both of them, and Louise leaned back against the sofa cushions as they hugged each other tightly.

It felt so strange to her.

Both of them consoling the other.

As a mother, she'd felt that it was her responsibility to be there for her daughter.

Now, they were there for each other.

It felt good.

But she was also sad that her daughter seemed to have matured beyond her years.

"You know you can always talk to me about things, right?"

Jemma nodded, her tears wetting the front of Louise's blouse. "I don't want to make you sad."

"Nothing makes me sadder than knowing that you're hurting, Jemma. We can be there for each other and help each other."

"I know." Jemma's sniffles eased a little and Louies felt her daughter shift in her embrace.

"And now we have Gray."

Gray?

Louise looked over at Grayson and saw his face.

He was stunned.

Shocked.

And in a way, he looked like he was melting.

Jemma's hand was holding onto Gray's shirt sleeve.

Against his thick arm, her daughter's hand looked smaller than it should.

Jemma's fingers gripped the plaid flannel fabric and held tight, reminding Louise of what it used to look like when Jemma would hold on to her teddy as a little girl.

When she fell asleep holding onto the super-soft plush fabric, there was nothing that could pry her hand from its comforting surface.

Louise could feel Jemma falling asleep.

All of the sadness and tears, the emotional turmoil was weighing on all three of them, and Louise knew that she'd have to get Jemma into bed soon, or they'd have to sleep out there on the sofa.

She just wasn't strong enough to carry her growing daughter down the hall to her room.

Almost as if Grayson had read her mind, he looked at her with a soft smile. "If I could, I'd carry her for you, but-"

"I know." She smiled at him. "You've done so much tonight," she explained. "I don't know how I'll be able to thank you."

Louise felt a heavy warmth on her arm and felt Grayson's fingers gently squeeze her forearm.

"You don't have to, Lou... Jemma and you both deserve to be happy. If I can help. I want to."

She nodded at him and managed a wavering smile in his direction. "You've done so much, already." She shifted on the sofa, moving toward the edge before she sat up fully. "Let me get her to bed."

Somehow, she got to her feet. Jemma was getting bigger by the day, so she felt her knees almost buckle before she managed to stand up tall.

Louise only made it a few steps away when Jemma lifted her head and looked back over her shoulder.

"Gray?"

Louise grinned at the new nickname.

"Yeah, Jem?"

"Can we keep reading tomorrow night?"

She didn't see Grayson's reaction, but she felt that question deep in her own chest.

She also felt hope rising up inside of her, racing with joy.

When she heard his answer, his voice was deeper, louder than she expected.

Then she felt a little additional weight on her shoulder and a soft shake.

Leaning her head to one side, she saw Grayson's finger rumpling Jemma's hair.

"Of course we can, Jem. Of course we can."

Jemma sagged against her shoulder. "Okay, mom. I'm ready to go to sleep."

"All right, sweetheart. Let's get you tucked in."

## – BIG 'N BURLY DUO 3 –

He didn't go into Jemma's room to watch Louise put her to bed, but he walked halfway down the hall and leaned against the wall, massaging his knee over the sleeve.

When he'd been injured, he felt the loss of his competitive career as if he'd lost the leg instead of having it broken.

Not being able to compete at rodeos in the future felt like he'd lost some of his purpose.

He'd always been eager to get to the next rodeo.

Take the next ride.

It wasn't about the buckles or the prize money so much as the adrenaline that coursed through his veins when he swung up into the saddle.

After his injury, he felt like that was lost to him forever.

He felt like it made him less than a man.

Less than he'd been for his whole life.

And now?

Standing there in the hallway, unable to carry that precious child into her bedroom and tuck her in without risking his recovery, made him feel like half a man.

He heard Louise whispering to her daughter, the two offering their nightly prayers together. He listened and he heard heart.

He heard love.

Love that he wanted to be a part of.

Just a few minutes before, he'd held Jemma as she'd cried and mourned her father.

And then he'd handed her to her mother and had the honor of watching the truest form of love expressed between a mother and child.

It was just that simple and that amazing.

Grayson leaned against the wall, feeling weary and the exhaustion set into his bones.

He was getting old.

Too old to be left standing on the outskirts of the kind of love he'd been witness to.

That wasn't really the issue upsetting him.

It wasn't just witnessing it and not being a part of it. It was not being a part of their family.

Yes, it had been a couple of weeks with Louise and Jemma living in his home, but he was a man used to making decisions in seconds.

Riding.

Roping.

Both activities came down to microseconds. Take one second too long to make a decision and you could find yourself breathing in dirt.

Or you could find yourself under the hooves of an angry animal more than happy to gore you or stomp you to death.

Wanting to be a part of their family was pure instinct and need, but it was still disconcerting as fuck.

Grayson had family throughout his life.

He'd loved his parents and a few grandparents who had lived long enough to make a life-long impression on his heart and soul.

And he still had John in his life and John's growing family, but none of those relationships had been his choice.

They were family that he'd been born into or chosen by others.

Louise.

Jemma.

He wanted them to be a part of his life.

Live in his home.

And that scared him.

It frightened him in a way that only one moment had up until he'd met the two ladies down the hall.

The accident had brought him face to face with death, but meeting Louise and spending time with her and her daughter had given him a taste of a life that he'd never imagined could be possible.

The light in the room dimmed and Grayson stayed there, watching the doorway for a long moment, until Louise stepped out into the hall.

She didn't have any idea that he was watching her.

He could tell that by the way she lifted up a hand to pull the tie from her hair.

The soft waves that he'd only seen a time or two in the last few weeks came down, swishing just above her shoulders.

He didn't want to admit how much his fingers ached to free that tie from her hair.

Grayson wanted to run his finger through her hair, comb it back from her face and someday wrap her hair around his fingers and tug her head back so his lips could touch her neck.

He'd always believed that he was like a lot of men. He wasn't a breast man, nor an ass man. He liked all of a woman's parts.

But there was something about Louise's neck.

It might be the loose ends of her hair that tickled the sides of her neck.

Lord knows he liked watching her across the room as she cleaned dishes in the sink. The soft light coming from the fixture above the sink cast its glow over her.

It lit the soft planes of her skin against the dark waves of her hair.

And thank fuck for the blanket that he left in the living room. He'd pulled that over himself more than a few times when he'd gotten ridiculously hard from just the sight of her neck.

He knew what her scent was like. They moved around each other almost effortlessly in the kitchen and living areas of the house.

It was during those times that he'd leaned in to catch a breath of her scent.

Soft, clean and gentle.

Her scent haunted him at night.

Grayson often woke up in the middle of the night from a dream where he held her tightly in his embrace, his face buried into the side of her neck, her body bare and breathtaking wrapped around his larger form.

And the sounds she made when he was throbbing deep inside of her.

"Ohhh."

Fuck.

Just like that.

The soft light in the room from Jemma's nightlight, lit her from behind and he could see the hand she held against her neck.

He couldn't see if her face was tense or tight from pain, but he could hear the ache in her tone.

"You want me to help with that?"

"Oh!" Louise's eyes opened and met his gaze from a few feet away. "Sorry, I didn't think you were out here."

"I wanted to wait for you."

"Really?"

He thought he heard a smile in her voice, but his eyes were fixed on her neck. She was rubbing the back of her neck.

"I might not be all that quick on my feet, but I've got strong hands."

She leaned back, her eyes widening. "I'm sorry, what?"

Grayson knew he should probably back off of the offer, but if he was being truthful to himself, he really wanted to touch her.

Nothing intimate, he knew.

But he had a feeling that he could relieve some of the pain in her neck and get a chance to breathe in her scent.

It might just be some kind of personal punishment on his part, but he was willing, *no*, more than willing to suffer for the opportunity to touch her again.

"Your neck. You look like it's hurting you."

She shrugged and lowered her hand, but the gesture looked like it hurt as well. "Jemma's growing like a weed. I bet she's going to grow out of her pants in a month or so." She sighed. "We'll have to look for a place where we can buy some clothes to get her through the growth spurt."

Louise hesitated, and he wondered what she'd been about to say.

There were things they didn't talk about.

He'd tried to talk about her plans after the summer, but Louise had been closed-lipped about it. Grayson wasn't sure if he understood her reticence to hold things back from him.

He'd have no problem listening to her or offering his help.

Maybe she just didn't understand that.

Yet.

"Why don't we sit down, and I'll see if I can help you with that pain in your neck."

Louise looked at him in a quizzical way and just when he was sure she would turn him down and excuse herself, she started to laugh.

Her easy-going laughter had him laughing along with her.

He shook his head. "How do you do it?"

She had her hands covering her mouth. "Do what?"

"Laugh like this." He gestured at her. "You amaze me, Lou. You can laugh at the drop of a hat and in that moment, I think you've gone over the edge."

"But..." She grinned at him. "I hope there's a but in there."

He'd love to talk about her butt, or touch it, but this wasn't the time. Instead, he gestured for her to move closer to him.

"You start to laugh and suddenly the whole mood in the room changes. Things are lighter. Easier. More relaxed."

Before he could stop himself, he lifted a hand and trailed his knuckles gently across her cheek.

"Things are more... you."

"Me?" She waved him off and started to walk toward the main room, slowing to let him walk beside her.

He was almost sure she had no idea that she was doing it. She was just amazing. She had empathy and kindness as a part of her genetic makeup.

If opposites attract, then Louise was his exact opposite.

Crazy?

Absolutely.

But he was quickly finding out that crazy was likely just what he needed.

Because he wanted her. And the whole amazing package that she came with.

"So, what do you think, Lou? Straight to bed? Or will you let me try to get rid of some of your pain?"

He saw the hesitation in her expression, but a moment later, her shoulders dropped, and her smile eased a little. "I can't pass up a massage, can I?"

"It's all up to you, Lou. But I think I can help."

"Okay." She nodded at him, smiling. "Sounds good to me."

Grayson gestured toward the main room and followed her. "Let's find a comfortable place for you to sit."

"I think that'll be half the fun," she stopped and turned to look at him with another devastating smile, "just having some quiet time with you."

## CHAPTER ELEVEN

### Roped by the Dad Bod

For days after, Louise would find herself stopping what she was doing and drifting off into her own thoughts, her hands rubbing over her shoulders or trailing her fingers across the back of her neck.

It was crazy, really.

It was just... a massage.

He was being kind.

He had been there to help her when she was struggling with her emotions as well as the pain in her back and shoulders.

That's all it was.

At least, that's what she told herself.

Her mind understood that.

Her body?

Her body ached for more.

Her emotions were distracting her during her work. Not enough that she wasn't getting everything done, but in those moments where she'd had free time and read her books.

She was now daydreaming about Grayson. About the warmth in his hands. The slightly raspy touch of his calluses against her skin. The way he seemed to know exactly where to press and how hard to touch her.

Those feelings?

Those thoughts?

They were still with her days later.

And she wasn't sure she'd ever forget his touch.

As she stood at the sink, she watched John's truck move down the drive. There was something exciting happening down at the barn, he'd explained. And Jemma, eager to help and spend time around the horses, jumped at the chance to go.

While Jemma was changing for the barn, John had checked in with Louise and let her know that they'd be paying Jemma for her work at the barn.

When Louise had tried to talk him out of it, she didn't get far.

It was only when he gave a look that she recognized as a 'Brandt' thing, that she realized it was futile to argue with either of the Brandt brothers.

Jemma had no idea about the arrangement. John understood that it was something Louise wanted to keep secret.

Jemma was helping at the barn because she truly enjoyed it. She was growing leaps and bounds, not just in her confidence, but in her personality.

Louise realized that her daughter had been too reserved for too long.

As the dust down the road began to settle, she sighed and shook her head.

Was that her own problem?

Had she been too quiet, too hesitant in her own life?

Too busy surviving to really and truly live?

A wind blew across the ground outside. She could see it in the dust that it stirred up going across the window and the bend and sway of some of the young trees that had been planted down the driveway.

It was likely hot outside. Summer, she laughingly reminded herself, got hot. And that wind, right at that moment, might feel pretty good.

Leaning one hand on the edge of the sink, she lifted her other and touched the back of her neck. It was cool inside the house, but outside the temperature against the back of her neck might be warm enough to feel like his hands were on her again.

Slowly, she moved the palm of her hand across the nape of her neck and felt strands of her hair catch in between her fingers.

The gentle pull of her hair made her smile. Tight-lipped and tender, she wondered if it might just happen again.

It was dangerous.

It was dangerous because she wanted it like she wanted her next breath.

It had been so long since she'd felt someone touch her with that kind of gentle strength that she ached for it again.

Sitting on the ottoman in front of the sofa, tucked carefully between his legs, she'd been only too conscious of her surroundings.

The inside of his thigh against her hip, the pressure she'd felt as he leaned into the massage.

And every once in a while, the warm heat of his breath on her neck.

The memory was keen, causing her body to react as if she was there with him again. She couldn't stop the way her breasts grew heavier with want, or the way her nipples tightened into tender points. She certainly couldn't tell herself not to ache between her legs or grow wet with need.

Not when every night that she was alone, she woke up

staring at the ceiling until she gave into temptation and let her hands move over her skin.

One hand playing over her sensitive breasts and the other slipping into her shorts until her fingers curled in the growing heat between her folds and ending with her fingers pinched around her clit as she turned her face into her pillow to hide the ragged gasp of her release as it was pushed from her throat.

And every night, he was there. Not just in her imagination, but on the other side of the wall.

He was also in her day dreams, her wandering mind.

If he was seated on the sofa, his leg propped up on the table, she'd think of how she might get herself to fit on his lap.

Was there room for her knees on either side of his hips?

Would she be able to feel him inside of her without causing him pain?

Would he even want her to be on his lap?

Hunger to suck her breast into his mouth, tongue her painfully tight nipples and make her beg to-

"Lou?"

Her chin dropped to her chest and when she opened her eyes just a hint, she could see the tight points of her nipples poking against the thin fabric of her tank top.

The thin cotton bra underneath it did nothing to hold them back. If she turned around, he'd likely see her needy state.

"Louise? You okay?"

"Fine." She answered him too quickly. A little too forcefully. "I'm," Louise shook herself at the thought and struggled to relax her tone and her body, "I'm fine. Sorry. I was just dozing off, I guess."

"I think you're working too hard if you're falling asleep on your feet. Come on over to the couch and sit down."

She was ready to shrug off his suggestion until his hand touched her shoulder.

It was a simple, innocent touch, but the need in her body roared to the forefront of her mind.

And other parts of her body.

She kept trying to tell herself that her physical reaction to him was just that. She'd been alone so long that her body was leaping at any chance to feel those kinds of sensations again.

Her mind was eager to jump to those conclusions, but her body told another story entirely.

It hungered for him.

It was his body that her own wanted, but it was the man he was on the inside that made her laugh and smile more than not.

He listened to her, and he asked her questions and let her lay her head on his shoulder when she needed his support.

Yes, she wanted his body and the pleasure she knew they could bring each other, but she wanted the man too.

There he was, right behind her, but she was too scared to turn around and let him see the want in her eyes.

What if he didn't feel the same way?

What if-

"Louise? Honey, you're worrying me."

Before she could steel herself, she felt his hand on her hip.

The soft tap of sound, she reasoned, was him laying his cane against the cabinet to her side.

When she drew in her next breath, she felt his arm brush up against her side and looking down she saw his hand take hold of the edge of the sink.

"Did I do something wrong?"

Did he... what?

"No," she shook her head, "nothing wrong. I'm just-"

"Just what, Louise?"

She froze in place, the heat of his breath fanned against her neck.

"It... It's nothing bad, I promise."

"Good." The hand on her hip gave her a little squeeze and that tender touch sent her mind into a needy spiral, her body adding its own eagerness into the mix. "I want to be responsible for the good stuff."

The good stuff.

Her mind instantly brought up an image of what they must look like.

His large body pressed up against hers, trapping her between himself and the sink.

A quick check of her height told her that she wasn't tall enough to bend over the sink, but-

"Louise. Tell me..." He moved closer, bringing the thigh of his good leg against the back of hers and that hard length she felt against her? Well, there was no way to miss what that was. "Am I crazy, honey? Am I the only one here feeling this... this thing between us?

"If I am, just say so and I'll stop. I'll even beg your damn forgiveness, because I don't want you to go away until you absolutely have to."

The hand on her hip turned slightly until his hand slid just under the hem of her tank top.

She could feel his thumb against her belly.

She knew she had to give him an answer. The last thing she wanted was for him to pull away. To regret the heat and comfort he was offering to her.

"Gray?" Her voice shook and her nipples tightened even more. "Gray?"

"Tell me, honey. Tell me what you want, because I know what I want. I hope to heaven that they're the same thing."

Louise tried to use her words. She wanted to answer him

with something akin to intelligent thought, but her body had other ideas.

Arching her back, she felt his hard length press against her lower back.

He wanted her. She could feel it.

She heard his soft exhale as he rocked his cock against her through his jeans and her shorts.

"Is that it, Lou? You want me like I want you?" The hand he had against her belly slowly skimmed up and over her ribs, coming to rest with the side of a finger under her breast.

A soft whimper escaped her lips.

"Tell me, Lou." She felt his finger sweep over the bottom curve of her breast. "Tell me if you want me as much as I want you."

Words failed her.

She wanted to say it. She wanted to give him the answer he wanted, but it felt like her heart was in her throat, keeping her from uttering a word.

So she turned around.

Careful for his healing leg, she managed to turn so she could look him in the eye and hopefully he'd see in her own gaze what her answer was.

But Grayson waited for her.

His arousal didn't dim. She felt it even more pressed against the soft curve of her belly. The hand that had touched her breasts so gently was on her lower back.

His gaze moved over her face as if he was committing it to memory.

"Cat got your tongue, honey? Or don't you want me to touch you like this?"

His hand slid lower on her back, encouraging her to rock into him and feel his unmistakable need for her.

Again, her voice failed her, but she had a feeling that she could prove it to him some other way.

Louise lifted her hands and set them on his powerful shoulders.

He was so thick in his chest and arms, and, she thought with a smile, his thighs too.

Her hands smoothed over his shoulders and then over the hard planes of his pecs. Lower they went until she felt the softer sides of his body, her hands going lower still until she leaned forward and gently grabbed a hold of his butt.

It was so beyond what she was comfortable with she felt her cheeks heat with the rush of blood, but she wasn't done there.

Leaning in, she pressed her lips against his.

The first kiss seemed to surprise them both, but the second and the third traded back and forth between the two of them as they silently debated who might be the one in charge.

Then it seemed that Grayson had won. His tongue slipping between her lips to tangle with her own. The scratch of his beard against her skin wasn't all that bad.

In fact, its texture left a broad path of sensation where it touched.

For a moment, because a moment was all that she could spare, she imagined what it might be like to feel his beard against the sensitive skin of her inner thighs.

She moaned into his mouth and Grayson doubled his efforts, his tongue mating with hers as their teeth clashed from time to time.

It was nearing the point that they might need a little more privacy.

Louise didn't expect anyone coming up the driveway.

Jemma would be down at the barn for a few more hours, but there was always a possibility that someone might see.

"Where?"

He opened his eyes to meet her gaze. "Where?"

"Uh." She nipped her teeth against her lower lip before she spoke again. "Do you want to come to my room?"

The words were foreign on her tongue.

When she'd been intimate with her husband, things had just worked.

This was different.

There was a kind of desperation that she felt to have his man inside of her.

The nerves in her body, especially the ones that led to the more pleasurable spots on her skin, were already buzzing with need.

He grinned at her. "If you mean to take me into your room so you can have your way with me, honey? Go right on ahead." Grayson raked his gaze all the way down her body and back up again. "Just know that I want to get my hands and mouth all over your body."

His words sent shivers of passion throughout her whole body.

"Okay," she was amazed that she found her voice when her breath was caught in her throat, but she wasn't going to hold back now. "Then you should come with me."

He reached for his cane, but she took his hand in hers and set it on her shoulder.

"You can lean on me."

# CHAPTER TWELVE

## Roped by the Dad Bod

He'd never felt more like an invalid than when Louise helped him shed most of his clothes.

While he'd been living in jeans with one leg sliced open to make for easy dressing, it certainly strained his ego to have her help him out of his pants as he laid there on the bed.

It was a struggle, as it took a bit of wiggling it around to get them off when the crown of his cock seemed to work against him, catching on the inside waistband of his jeans.

But his ego got a boost when she dropped his pants off the side of the bed and she turned back around to see his dick, thick and erect, jutting up at her.

Her gaze stayed fixed on him as she lifted the hem of her tank and when she pulled that off over her head, he fucking groaned.

Those pretty little points he'd seen pressing against her tank top had been easy to see, but straining against the worn cotton of her bra, they looked nearly obscene in the most amazing way.

He wanted his mouth on her.

He wanted his tongue tasting her.

And given the way his cock twitched and sent a drop of pre-cum sliding down its swollen head, he needed in her.

Grayson was on the verge of telling her to take off her bra and bottoms, but he couldn't say a word.

Louise rose up on her knees and straddled his good leg. She held her gaze on his cock long enough to take it in her hand and then, as he watched, she bent over and kissed it.

It painted her bottom lip, and Grayson grabbed at the sheets near his hips.

He wanted to sit up and wrap his hand around the nape of her neck.

He wanted to lick his own arousal from her lips and then taste it again as he suckled on the tip of her breast.

"I want you so damn much."

He heard his own voice in his ears and knew how needy he sounded.

He couldn't care less about that.

Grayson wanted her to know.

And maybe she did, because she leaned over against him and as the tip of one of her pretty pear-shaped breasts dragged along his thigh, she took him in her mouth.

"Fuuuuck me."

His hands were fisted around his sheets, and he forced them to stay there.

Need rode him so hard that he was tempted to thread his fingers through her hair and help her take him deeper.

But what she was doing to him felt so damn good already.

"Your mouth," he ground out the words between clenched teeth, "feels like... heaven."

She said something, or she hummed. Either way, his hips bucked up, eager to feel that same sensation again.

Ten times.

A hundred.

Then he felt it.

That prickle of electricity along his spine.

No.

No!

He didn't want it to end like this.

Not so fast.

Grayson cursed himself in his thoughts. This wasn't how he wanted her to remember their first time.

And it would only be their first.

So he pried his fingers from the sheets and reached for her. "Stop. Please, Louise. Stop."

She looked back at him with a grin, and he'd never seen her look so vibrant and wild as she was in that moment.

He was tempted to let her take him over the edge. He'd make it better for her the next time and the-

"Gray! Louise?"

They both froze as they heard someone calling their names.

Louise turned to look at him and he saw the question in her eyes.

"That's Laney."

She nodded. She'd probably recognized the voice, but neither one of them was thinking clearly.

"Hey, where are you guys?"

Grayson started to move on the bed, but a stab of pain went through his leg.

Louise reached out and touched his knee.

He could see that she was torn.

One of them had to go out and talk to Laney.

"Can you wait here?"

Louise looked up at him, searching his eyes for the answer.

"Yeah. I'm good." He reached his hand down and rubbed at his leg above the compression sleeve. He knew it would take him longer to get dressed than she would.

Louise slid from the bed and picked up her tank and shorts, dressing as she walked toward the door.

"Laney?" She gave him a rueful little grin as she reached for the door. "I'm coming out."

## - BIG 'N BURLY DUO 3 -

Louise stepped into the hallway and saw Laney's hand on the knob of Grayson's bedroom door.

"Sorry, I was getting dressed."

Laney nodded, but the motion was a little hesitant. "Is everything okay?"

"Sure!" Louise clenched her teeth together, her voice was a little too bright. "Sorry, I'm a little out of breath."

Laney's perfect eyebrows raised. "Do you need to sit down?"

Louise waved off her concern. "Nothing like that. I was just... busy doing something in my room."

Laney leaned against the wall, gracefully folding her arms across her chest. "Something."

If she wasn't already a little hot and bothered, she might not have started to sweat under Laney's curious gaze.

"Where's Gray?"

"Wow." She winced. That word shouldn't have escaped from her lips. "Uh, he's got a leg cramp."

Laney leaned over so she could look into the living room. "Well, I should... let you guys take care of that... cramp."

Laney started to move around her toward the door and Louise realized what Laney was talking about.

"Laney, I-"

Turning back around to look at her, Laney waved off her excuse. "No need to explain, Louise. I'm... I'm not exactly surprised."

"Wait, what?" Louise met her halfway across the hardwood floor. "Laney-"

Laney grabbed her hand and Louise was so embarrassed that her hand was shaking. "If you're worried about what I'm thinking, don't be."

Lifting her free hand, Louise placed her palm against the side of her neck, wondering if Laney would see the blush that she still felt on her skin.

There was only natural light in the room, but the room was still well lit. It wouldn't be hard to see the reddish blush on her skin.

"I only stopped by because you two weren't answering your phones. John thought you might need an extra pair of hands, but I don't think John would expect me to help with this."

Louise thought she was going to die of embarrassment.

"We thought of coming over tonight to bring some dinner and have a little family event."

She almost leapt at the idea. "That's fine! More than fine." Louise let out a breath. "I'll be happy to warm things up or I can cook for all of you. Jemma and I can set the table and serve at the table."

Laney drew back and shook her head. "I'm not expecting you to serve at the table."

Louise shrugged and started to talk, but Laney rushed ahead of her. "You and Jemma are basically family. I meant that we'd all sit down together, but I really need to ask Gray. I don't want him to fuss that we just invited ourselves to dinner."

That's where Louise found herself teetering back and forth between panic and abject horror.

Laney could clearly see that Gray wasn't in the main room and she would easily be able to see that he wasn't in his bedroom.

Even if he called out, Laney would know that Gray was in her room.

This could turn out into a horrible mess.

"I could ask Gray after... after his nap and he'll let you know."

"Nap?"

Louise could tell that Laney wasn't buying the excuse. She could feel the blood draining from her face.

"You went into his room."

She didn't make it a question. She didn't need to. The look on Laney's face was enough of an answer.

"It's..." She sucked in a breath as her mind struggled to come up with something to say that didn't sound like a total lie. "It's not-"

"Laney!"

Louise dropped her head until her chin touched her chest.

It was only a moment before she felt Laney's hand touch her arm. It was a squeeze first and then a pat.

"Leave her alone, Laney."

"You, uh... okay in there, Gray?"

Louise heard Laney's smiling tone and couldn't help the smile that touched her lips.

She was still embarrassed as hell, but Laney wasn't upset. She didn't even seem shocked.

"Don't push this, Laney. Leave Louise alone, okay?"

Laney shook her head. "Hey! I'm not a jerk! If you two are getting to know each other, I'll be thrilled." She turned around and gave Louise a wink. "Are you going to be a grouch if we come up for dinner tonight?"

"You're gonna do what you're gonna do, Laney. Let's just keep this private."

"Private, meaning that I can't tell John about the two of you?"

Louise wanted to bury her head in the sand and insist that she stay in her room during dinner, but that wasn't about to happen.

Laney took Louise's hand in her own and met her gaze as she spoke. "John was the one who saw things changing between you two. So he'll see it all on his own."

Laney pulled her into a hug, and it took Louise a moment for her to lift her arms and return the hug.

When she pulled back, she was grinning ear to ear. "I'm not trying to make you feel bad or embarrassed, Louise. If you and Gray work out together, I'm going to be so happy."

Turning toward the hall, Laney cupped her hands around her mouth. "I'm headed home. We'll text when we're coming up, so one of you should have your cell phone nearby. Later, brother!"

She was gone a moment later and Louise barely managed to hold herself together.

She wasn't a young woman anymore, but heaven help her, pride didn't seem to matter much anymore.

The few moments that she'd been with Grayson, she was a different person. Her blood pulsed through her body, both taking her breath and making her heart pound at the same time.

She'd felt young again.

She'd felt passion again.

And knowing that Grayson found her attractive?

It was a gift.

Even better than that was how he treated Jemma. He'd become someone who Jemma liked to talk to. Someone Jemma asked questions of without fear that he'd send her away.

No, she wasn't expecting him to pick up where her husband had left off, but he gave them both his time and attention and that, as far as she was concerned, was better than gold.

"Lou?"

Startled, Louise had to clear her throat before she could speak. Her emotions, it seemed, had been bottled up inside.

"Y-yes?"

"Can you help me get dressed?"

She nodded and then spoke aloud. "Sure. I'll be right in."

Louise wasn't upset at all.

The mood had been broken, but she was determined not to turn it into something weird.

She'd help Grayson get dressed and then she'd message Laney and find out what she could cook ahead of dinner to make things easier for their guests.

## CHAPTER THIRTEEN

## Roped by the DAD BOD

Dinner turned out to be better than he expected.

Sure, Grayson knew that Jemma got along with Laney and John. She'd probably get alone with anyone if they had half a brain to see how great a kid she was.

But there he was, watching her at the table with his family, engaged and engaging with everyone. Smiling and giggling and helping Laney with the kids, even though she was still a kid herself.

Louise sat beside him, taking in the scene with her eyes wide and her heart on her sleeve.

It humbled him to realize that the family he loved and considered as perfectly normal and, in a way, commonplace, was amazing to her.

Just as she was amazing to him.

"Hey, Gray!"

Grayson looked down the table at his brother, John. "Yes?" John had always ribbed him at every opportunity. When they were both grown, John told him that he needed to do it to keep him humble and down to earth.

He hoped that the look in his eyes was enough to deter John from ribbing him too hard with Louise and Jemma at the table.

It was the first time in years that Grayson cared what his brother might say, because, for the first-time in... forever, he cared what people thought about him outside of the Rodeo arena.

John lifted up his glass of water and gave a little nod. "You look happy, man. I'm glad to see it."

Grayson was half-expecting his brother to make fun of him. Instead, he'd turned Grayson's worry on its head.

Grayson lifted his glass, mirroring his brother. "I am happy, John. Thanks."

Before he set his glass down, he took a sip and saw Jemma move out of the corner of his eye. She'd chosen the seat on one side of him when they got to the table and now, she lifted her glass to him before she took a sip of her own.

She didn't say a word, but Grayson saw the light in her eyes and the white of her teeth as she grinned.

In reflex, Grayson turned to look at Louise and found her near tears.

Her gaze was turned toward her daughter and he saw the joy beyond the tears.

Then, as if she'd just caught on to the fact that he was looking at her, she lifted her gaze to his.

It staggered him. Thank God that he was sitting down because he might have fallen over with the way his heart shifted inside of his chest.

The brazen smile she'd treated him to a few hours ago had softened into a look of maternal love, but now, as she looked at him, he thought he saw an emotion somewhere in between.

Joy. Hope.

Love?

Crazy as it might seem to himself and his family, he really hoped it was love.

Not just because he was on the receiving end of it, but because he wanted to know if she was open to receiving it.

He reached out and covered her hand with his, giving it a gentle squeeze before he leaned closer. "What about you, Lou? How are you feeling?"

She darted a look at her daughter, and he turned to look as well.

Jemma was using a tiny spoon to scoop up some baby food off of the baby's chin while they both laughed.

"I feel... I feel so happy after such a long time."

Grayson turned back to Louise and saw her turn her gaze to him.

"I thought we were okay but being here and seeing her laugh and smile more than anything else, has really shown me that we could have been doing so much better."

"You've done so much for Jem, Louise. You're an incredible mother."

The light in her eyes was mesmerizing.

Her beautiful face was alight and glowing. He wanted to give her this kind of joy every day for the rest of his life.

"You're an amazing woman, too."

He'd taken her by surprise. He could see that in the way her expression changed.

From happy, to thoughtful, to happy again.

He wanted to pull her in his arms and tell her that he'd do everything to make her life and Jemma's the best that it could be, but that wasn't something to say at a crowded table.

He wanted to offer her the world, but she deserved time to think about it. Time to understand that his quick turnaround had everything to do with how he felt deep down inside.

Instead of feeling like she had to react because she was in front of an audience.

And waiting wasn't something he liked.

Even at a rodeo. He'd wait for his time, but he'd wait with his pulse pounding until the moment the gate opened. Then his heartbeat would slow, counting off the seconds in time to the seconds on the clock.

This moment was different in one incredibly important way.

At a rodeo, he was in his wheelhouse. He knew that he could get that rope around a calf's hooves. The calf's neck. He could do whichever role he needed to and do it like he was born to it.

Talking to Louise about their next step... their future was something else entirely.

He didn't know if he'd be able to say something romantic. Hell, he didn't even know if he'd say something intelligible.

He just knew that he'd had his heart opened by Louise and her daughter.

Now, he just had to find a way to make them feel the same way so that they'd want to stay.

## – BIG 'N BURLY DUO 3 –

He was holding her hand.

Well, he was covering her hand.

It wasn't something that normally happened to her. Even though she'd loved and been loved by her husband, he hadn't been big at public displays of affection.

As they continued their meal, Grayson rarely lifted his hand away from hers.

And when he did, he brought it right back again.

Louise wasn't sure what emotions had settled in her chest, but she did know one thing.

She really liked the feelings that he brought up inside of her.

Grayson Brandt wasn't like her former husband. She'd married her high school sweetheart. They'd been each other's firsts. First kiss. First Love. First lover.

It had been expected that they would marry and marry they did. And been happy together.

This... whatever *this* was between herself and Grayson, was new territory for her.

First, it was her attitude from the beginning.

Adversity hadn't been her strong suit when she met Jemma's father. She'd crumbled over bad grades. She'd stressed over simple things.

It wasn't until she was pregnant with Jemma that she started to stand a little taller, emotionally.

She became resilient because she had to for her daughter's sake.

When she'd met Grayson, she'd come prepared for a battle.

She'd been warned that he might be... difficult.

She wasn't planning on being difficult back to him. She'd planned on meeting him head on and changing his mind.

Then, as she'd gotten to know Grayson better. As she'd seen him with Jemma and heard how warm he'd been with her daughter, Louise had opened her heart instinctively toward Grayson.

Then it was how much she came to care for him.

She was fascinated by him and the more she learned, the more she liked.

It didn't hurt that sometimes she'd turn and see him watching her.

She'd seen the heat in his eyes and the way his hands flexed, as if he didn't know what to do with his hands.

She'd felt the same way during their weeks together.

The way she'd sneak glances at him when he was reading quietly, or talking to Jemma.

The broad set of his shoulders, the thick muscles of his legs and arms. Then, there was the way he filled out a pair of jeans.

One leg cut up past his knee so that he could wear it over his fracture boot didn't change the way those jeans clung to the rest of him.

And his chest. Goodness! His chest.

She'd never realize how much she'd like a man who was thick all over. He was like a big growly teddy bear and those growls made her feel like she could feel the vibrations against her skin.

Nearly every night after that, she'd gone to sleep only to come face to face and skin to skin with that same man.

The way he touched her in her dreams had almost become a reality a few hours before.

She wanted to feel that again.

It was a drugging feeling for her to realize how powerful she'd felt with him in bed. How much freedom she'd felt to explore sensations with him. Taking him in her mouth had been a true rush of feeling.

Grayson Brandt was not a soft man by any definition, but he'd given her control. He'd told her how much she'd made him feel. How vulnerable he was with her.

That, in itself, was a gift.

And just before dinner, when she'd gone into her shared bathroom with Jemma to freshen up, she'd seen the woman in the mirror and realized that she was…

Different.

A good kind of different.

She just hoped that it would continue on like that after they left the ranch.

## CHAPTER FOURTEEN

### Roped by the Dad Bod

After dinner, Jemma was exhausted and barely managed to change into her nightgown before she fell, face first into her pillows. Louise managed to laugh silently as she maneuvered her daughter's form so that she could sleep with all of her limbs on the bed.

She sat there for a moment, watching Jemma smiling as she slept, before getting up and turning toward the door.

Grayson was standing there, watching her.

She met him in the doorway, standing where he was leaning against the frame.

"I've never seen her so tired."

Louise nodded. "She wore herself out between all of the talking and playing with the baby."

"Are you tired?"

His question caught her unawares.

"I'm... tired, but I'm not... I'm not ready to go to bed yet."

His eyes opened wider at her last word. "What are you in the mood for?"

She took a breath and then answered him with all of the courage she had behind her words.

"I'd like to spend some time with you."

His smile sent tingles throughout her body, and she lifted her hand to touch the side of his face.

Grayson turned his head and his lips brushed against her palm. Added together with the soft rasp of his beard, she leaned into his touch.

"I want to spend time with you, too." The look in his eyes was open and blatantly heated. "I want to kiss you senseless."

Louise felt her cheeks grow hot and she moved closer to whisper in his ear. "Then let's find somewhere we can do that."

After she closed Jemma's door, he wrapped an arm around her waist, and they moved into the main room of the house.

It was quiet in there. The only light coming in through the kitchen windows was from the moon.

When they came within a few feet of the sofa, she turned and brushed her lips against his cheek.

"Go ahead." She smiled at both the thoughts in her head and her ability to voice them. "You sit first."

Louise wasn't sure if he understood what she meant, but he didn't argue.

He sat down and she helped him bolster his leg on the sofa with extra cushions. She wanted to make sure that he was comfortable.

When she was done, he looked up at her with a question on his lips. "You look pretty proud of yourself. What's going on in your head?"

"Just thinking about how much I've dreamed about you."

He crooked a finger at her and reached for the waistband of her shorts.

His hand dropped down to his thigh as he watched her push her shorts down over her hips and to mid-thigh. That's when they fell from her fingers to make a thin little pile on the ground.

She doubted that he could see where they fell, but when her gaze met his, she saw that he was watching her, not her clothes.

Louise stepped out of her shorts and got up onto the sofa, moving carefully enough that she didn't hurt him.

When she straddled his hips, she heard his sharp inhale.

"Anything sore?" She worried about him.

She worried about everyone she-

Louise stopped short of completing that thought. She didn't want to complicate things.

He reached for her hips and held her in place. His eyes seemed to darken as he pulled her down so she was flush against him. "Not sore. But aching." He rocked her against him. "For you."

The motion was enough to make her list a little, rocking her off balance.

She leaned forward and braced her hands on the arm of the sofa behind him.

"I think I'm aching for you, too."

He slipped his hands to her back and then down to cup her butt, and then he gave it a squeeze. "There's a remedy for that, you know?"

Oh, she knew that.

Her nipples were already keenly sensitive and had been since earlier in the day.

Ah, who was she kidding?

Every time she was around Grayson, she was sensitive and tingly all over her body.

She wanted to beg him for his touch, but instead she managed a little tease.

"I'm not sure if I know. Maybe you could... show me?"

Before she could second guess her words, Grayson tugged her closer and her arms bent as she held onto the sofa.

Grayson found her breast behind the cotton of her blouse, drawing the tip of it into his mouth.

The wet heat of his mouth worked its way through the fabric and the sensations he wrought were amazing, almost mind-numbing.

"I thought... Oh, wow. I thought," she began again when his teeth nipped at her, "that you wanted..."

His hands slipped under the hem of her shirt and his fingers swept over the sensitive skin along her sides.

She certainly wasn't ticklish now.

The fabric lifted along with his hands and with a quick and desperate thought, she sat up and pulled her top up and off of her body.

He sat up, his mouth finding her other breast, his tongue and teeth going to work with a passion she had never felt before.

Grayson broke away for a moment to look up into her eyes. She knew she was already dazed by their physical contact. The look in his eyes turned her blood into fire. "What were you saying, honey?"

Louise had to reach into her memory for the answer to that question.

"I... I was just wondering..."

He was already back at work, turning her mind to mush.

"... you said... Oh god. You said," her mind kept losing its grip on her thoughts, "that you... Ah, hell. Something about kissing."

He pulled his mouth from her breast again and he groaned, squeezing her thighs together.

Grayson moaned beneath her. "I love your thighs, Lou. I'm gonna need to get you riding on a horse."

She ground her hips against him. "I like what I'm riding right now."

She felt heat spread across the back of her neck at her saucy little comment. He brought out the wildness inside of her.

Louise caught sight of his hands moving between them and then she felt him snap open the clasp between her breasts.

"I said," he pulled the wet cups of cotton off of her breasts, "I wanted to kiss you senseless. I'd say I'm doing a pretty good job of it."

He cupped her breasts in his hands, using his fingers on one hand to pinch and pull at her nipple as his mouth did the same to the other side.

She arched her back, giving him better access to her breast and lightly dragging her sex over his erection.

*Oh, yes. That's what he'd said.*

Grinning to herself she rocked against him, over and over as his mouth and fingers lifted her higher and higher.

She bit into her bottom lip to keep from making noise.

Grayson moved his mouth from one breast to the other and the sensations of his mouth and his beard felt like it might just send up flames of passion to burn her alive.

"I love the way you feel." He circled her nipple with the tip of his tongue. "I love the way you taste."

"I loved your taste, too." A moment later, she gasped. "Oh!"

His dick felt even harder between her legs and her thoughts started to go silent in her head.

When he took his mouth off of her flesh again, she wanted to scream with frustration, but his words tempered her emotions.

"Lift up, honey. I need to feel how sweet you are inside."

Using the arm of the sofa, she leaned forward so she could get her weight over her hands.

When she felt his hand slip between her legs, she resisted the urge to draw her thighs closer together to press his fingers against her, but she let him have the room he wanted.

His fingers pushed the gusset of her panties to the side and a moment later, Louise felt him slide a couple of fingers into her pussy.

She almost came right then and there.

His fingers were thick like the rest of him, and it wasn't long before she was rocking over his hand and enjoying the thick push of his body inside of hers.

"Ride my fingers, Lou. And let me make you come."

Oh, that wasn't going to be hard at all.

His mouth on her, his fingers in her, it all led up to a perfect storm that had her breaking apart into a thousand shimmery pieces before she came to rest, laid out on his chest.

She couldn't even raise her head to ask. "Are we going to do this again? Because I really think I need to be mindless a little more often."

He rubbed his hand over the dewy skin of her back. "The more the better, Lou. The more the better. Now that I know what I've been missing. I want to make up for wasted time in my life."

She heard his heart pounding in her chest, grounding her to his rhythm.

She wasn't going to argue with him, not about this.

## CHAPTER FIFTEEN

### Roped by the Dad Bod

As the summer wore on, life for Grayson suddenly actually resembled the word. He woke up smiling at the scent of coffee in the air and rolled out of bed (gingerly) to hobble into the main room to find Jemma and Louise waiting for him at the table.

He was looking forward to his next doctor's appointment. He felt good.

Strong.

Grayson knew that he was ready to get out of using that crazy boot and get back to... everything.

He even felt like the hitch he had in his giddy-up was finally working itself out and it had a lot-

No.

It had everything to do with Louise and Jemma.

He sat down in his chair and caught Jemma's big grin directed at him.

"What's up, Jem?" He reached over and tousled her hair. "You looking forward to something?"

"Yep." She started to wipe milk off of her chin with the

back of her hand, but he caught her and put a napkin in her hand.

Louise cast an approving look in his direction and he felt like he was a rooster, puffing out his chest.

"I'm betting that by the time I get back from the stable, you'll be back from the doctor with all kinds of good news!" Jemma put her fist up in the air and crowed.

"Doctor?"

Louise set down a plate of sausages on the table.

"Are you going to the doctor today?"

"Yeah." He tried to brush it off, but Louise wasn't having it.

"Which doctor?"

Jemma giggled. "Mom! It's not Halloween!"

Grayson didn't know what to think when Louise's answering laughter to her daughter was less than heartfelt.

Louise gave her daughter's hand a gentle pat and turned to look at him again.

"What kind of doctor are you seeing today?"

"My orthopedic surgeon. He's taking a look at how I'm healing up. If he gives me the okay. I'm going to get this boot off of my leg."

"That..." She swallowed and smiled. "That's great news."

"Do you... I mean, would you want to come with me?"

"No." Louise turned around and faced the wall and windows.

Grayson looked at Jemma and saw that she was looking at him, too.

'What's wrong?' Jemma's whispered words were nearly silent, but he got her meaning.

'Don't know.' His answer had them both worried.

There was a knock at the side door on the other side of the mudroom.

"Okay, Mom. I'm headed over to the barn."

Jemma got up from the table, but stopped before she moved away to grab the napkin that Grayson had given her and wiped across her mouth, ending with a grin.

Louise was standing near the doorway and bent down to give her daughter a kiss. "All right, sweetie. You be wonderful again, okay?"

Jemma's shoulders shook with laughter. "You always say I'm wonderful!"

"Well, you just are, so deal with it."

Seconds later, he heard a pair of horses head off toward the stable on the property. Through the screen on the front door, he could see the horses riding off easily down the dirt road.

He sat back, his plate still empty, to look at the beautiful woman, avoiding his gaze.

"Lou? Honey?"

"Your plate is empty. You need to eat and keep up your strength."

He wanted to argue that he had more than enough food and his strength wasn't in question, but her words told him that she cared.

That was the first step.

He reached out his fork and picked up a piece of the sausage and worked it off his fork and onto his plate. "How did you know?"

"I can hear. And these forks against these plates make a good amount of noise. You need to eat before you go to the doctor."

He didn't like the strain in her voice. Not one bit.

He got out of his chair and hobbled around the table to talk to her, but she moved before he could.

When she was several feet away he called out to her.

"Lou! Stop! Please. Talk to me."

She stopped just shy of her bedroom door and after a long, shoulder lifting breath, she turned back around and looked at him.

"Okay. I stopped."

"What's going on? Why are you upset? Are you mad at me?"

"Mad? At you?" The look on her face wasn't anger, it looked closer to hurt. "No."

"Okay. Did I hurt you?"

Her cheeks blushed red. "No. You've never hurt me, even when we..."

He fought off the instinctive smile that came with that memory. Well, all of the memories that they'd made all over the house.

"Then tell me what has you ready to run from me."

"I'm not running from you."

He dropped his chin down and stared at her. "I'm calling bullshit. And I own half a ranch, honey. I *know* my bullshit."

She turned on her heel, facing away from him, and then turned back. "I'm not running. I'm just... I just need some time to think. I need some time to get my thoughts together. I need time to... Oh, it doesn't matter."

It hurt like fuck, but he caught up to her and grabbed onto her arm.

When she whirled around to face him, he didn't see a trace of anger on her face.

He saw tears.

"Aw, shit, Lou." He pulled her into his embrace and laid her head against his shoulder. "Tell me, honey. What's wrong?"

"It's senseless." He heard her voice sound too bright to be true. "It's all in my head and I just... I just need to get over it."

He blew out a breath, frustrated, but he still held her close.

"Okay. So you need to get over it. I can understand."

She nodded and tried to step back, but he continued to hold her. "Gray-"

"Look," he pressed a kiss to the crown of her head, "I wasn't going to bother you about taking me to the appointment, but-"

"No. No. Of course not, but-"

He let her lean back then, but only to grab her chin gently and kiss her into silence.

When she was good and dazed, he pulled away.

"Stop brushing everything off, honey. I want you to come with me to the doctor and one other errand. I'll have John drive us so you don't have to worry about anything other than wrapping that beautiful mind around what's going to happen today."

"So I just need to sit there?"

He grinned at her. "Something like that, but if you want to do something else, I'm good with that, too."

"Uh... okay?"

He lifted his hand and brushed her hair back from her face. "That's all I'm asking, Lou. Just come with me today."

## – BIG 'N BURLY DUO 3 –

Louise knew that she should have brought some duck tape with her. It was an old adage that she learned in high school theater class.

'If it's supposed to move and it doesn't - WD40. If it's not supposed to move and it does - Duck Tape.'

And her moving parts came from her heart as it was falling apart.

During the few months that she'd been there at the Brandt Ranch, she'd fallen hopelessly in love with Grayson Brandt.

Going to the doctor, she knew that he'd be given a chance to get out of the fracture boot and that meant that her days at the ranch were limited.

It wasn't just being upset for herself. Jemma loved helping out at the barn. She was excited for the barn cat who was about to have kittens and she was developing a lovely rapport with one of the rescued horses.

She'd have to find something to occupy Jemma wherever they ended up moving.

Oh god. That was a problem, too!

Sure, she'd been looking for a new place to live. Apartments seemed more cost effective and she'd need to save money so that Jemma could still have her riding lessons. Everyone said she could go far, really far with her riding with the proper training, and she wanted her daughter to have that.

The main problem was, nothing seemed to fit with the listings she'd looked at.

Some where in bad areas. Some were too expensive. Some didn't have access to basic services nearby like grocery stores and good schools.

And she knew that Jemma was just as in love with Grayson and the ranch as she was.

The other night, as Louise tucked her into bed, Jemma had told her a secret she'd been holding back. Jemma wished that Grayson could be her daddy. Not to replace her biological father, the man who'd been there for most of her life, but a dad for the rest of her life. A man who cared about her.

Louise understood. She secretly wanted Grayson, too, but

she didn't tell her daughter that. The last thing she wanted was to get her hopes up and now that Grayson might be getting out of his fracture boot, he wouldn't need her for much longer.

She would really have to buckle down and find some place where they would be safe enough to start over again.

It was crazy. Really.

She'd needed a place to live and a place to work. She really hadn't expected to fall in love.

## – BIG 'N BURLY DUO 3 –

The ride into town was a little tense, at least for her.

Grayson and John were exchanging barbs at each other. And jokes. They had a never ending supply of jokes.

Some of them were even good.

But she still barely managed a soft chuckle.

She could see the guys sharing looks in the rearview mirror, but Louise was barely holding it together as it was.

She couldn't deal with their worries, too.

As they entered the edge of town, Grayson leaned forward on the seat. "John? Can you turn down Ellinger, please?"

"Please?" The younger brother was chuckling at that. "You asked so nicely, so yes, I will turn down Ellinger. Are we going someplace... special?"

Grayson almost growled at his brother.

"Okay. Okay." John put on his signal and slowed down to make the turn on Ellinger.

Just a few minutes later, they were at a decent-sized strip mall with an assortment of businesses set up in the semicircle of storefronts.

"Can you drop me off at Lewis & Son?"

"I dunno," the younger teased, "can I?"

Grayson huffed at that answer. "Pull over at the curb or I'm going to throw you out of here to let you walk back!"

"Oh, wow. He's got something up his ass."

Louise didn't offer to get out, but Grayson held the door for her. There were cars coming up behind them or she wouldn't have gotten out.

She just didn't want to hold anyone up.

When they entered the shop, she saw a number of old fancy clocks on the walls of the shop. A few looked familiar to her. "Is this where you get all of your clocks?"

He looked at her with feigned shock. "Of course it is! Don't imply to Jay that we'd get them anywhere else."

The man who walked up to the counter shook his head. "I hope you're only telling the truth to this beautiful woman, Grayson."

He put his hand over his heart. "I'm doing my best."

"Funny." The other man waved his hand in the air. "But I know you're not here for the jokes." He held up his hand for patience. "It'll just be one moment."

Jay disappeared into the back and returned a moment later with a small blue velvet box. He set it on the counter and looked at Grayson.

"It's up to you what you want to do with it."

Grayson picked up the box and held it in his hands for a moment.

"When John married Laney, he gave her our mother's ring. He was our mother's favorite." He fiddled with the lid a bit before slowly opening it under her watchful gaze. "That's why I'm going to ask you to wear my grandmother's ring, Lou. Louise. My love."

He paused for a moment. "I should have gone to the

doctor's first so that I could maybe do the down-on-one-knee thing, but I didn't want you to wait through that and think that there was a chance of me letting you two go and live somewhere away from me."

Grayson held out the box and looked at her over the top of it.

"So, what do you say, Louise? Will you take pity on a grumpy bachelor and make him a husband and a father at the same time?"

She looked at him and then back at the ring, her lips pressed together in a thin, pale line.

"Lou?"

She gasped in a breath and covered her mouth with her hands.

"Honey?" Grayson turned the box around to look at the ring. "If you don't like the ring, I could-"

"Oh my god, it's not about the ring!" She clapped her hands over her mouth again, feeling tears welling up in her eyes before she lowered her hands again. "I was so worried that you didn't feel the same way! I didn't know how we'd stand it when it was time to leave you." She sucked in a breath and felt the edges of her vision darken a little. "I'm so glad that we don't have... that we don't need..."

"Louise? Are you okay?"

"Okay?" She swallowed and felt her mouth go dry and her stomach twist in her middle. "Oh no. I don't think I am." She looked up at Grayson and realized too late that she shouldn't have done it.

The room around her twisted and turned and finally it went dark.

. . .

She woke up in a softly lit room and when she turned on her side to see what was going on she saw Grayson sitting in a chair with both of his legs looking identical to each other.

No boot.

"Hey there," he got up from the chair and moved to her side, "you were so eager for me to get the all clear on my leg that you passed out in the store."

Her memories came roaring back in her head and she felt horrible.

"I'm so sorry. I don't know what happened! I think I might have had a panic attack or something like that."

His brow furrowed. "Do you have a lot of panic attacks?"

"No," she shook her head. "I did a few times before, but it was right after... right after we lost him. I wasn't eating a lot back then. I have a better grasp on everything now."

He nodded and slowly helped her raise the back of the hospital bed so that they could talk face to face. "I'm glad to hear that, but the doctor doesn't think it was a panic attack."

"Oh? Then what?"

He pointed at her arm and she saw a bandage wrapped around her elbow. "He took some blood and said he'd be back in a few minutes."

The doctor stepped in a few seconds later. "Ah," he began, "as usual. I have the best timing for the good stuff! Welcome back to the land of the conscious, Miss-"

"It's Louise, doctor. Please call me Louise."

"Well, Louise," he smiled at her, "I have your results here. And as I thought, you two have some great news."

"We?" Louise gestured between herself and Grayson. "What's that?"

"I hope you don't mind a few more months of dizziness from time to time, but here's hoping it might just be a one off."

"Doctor?" Louise felt her cheeks flush with color. "What are you-"

He handed over a paper printout, but Louise couldn't focus enough to read the paper.

She didn't have to.

She'd seen reports like that before.

"Wow," she looked at Grayson, "when you said you wanted to be a father, you really called it."

Before she could utter another word, Grayson had the box out and open before her. "Please, honey. Before one of us faints at the news, I need an answer. Are you marrying me?"

"Of course, you big, growly goof! You're stuck with us now."

Grayson let out a breath. "Thank god!" He put the ring on her finger and gently wrapped his arms around her. "If you didn't say yes, I was going to have to figure out how to talk you into it."

"And goodness knows," she looked down at the ring and then back up into his gorgeous face, "you're not always the best guy with words."

"True. So true, honey."

"So," Louise made some space for him to sit beside her on the bed, "if I hadn't agreed, what would be your next plan?"

He grinned at her and she loved the contrast with his smile and his dark beard.

"Well, now that I have my cast off, I was planning to get back to what I do best."

She narrowed her gaze at him.

"What's that?"

"I'm a roper, honey. I was going to come after you with a lasso every time you tried to leave."

"You were going to rope me?"

His grin was even wider. "Over and over, as long as it took for me to find the words to convince you to stay."

"Well, you're in luck. It will only take you three words."

"Three." He nodded and leaned in for a kiss. "I love you, Louise."

She grinned back at him. "That's four."

He shook his head and groaned. "I think I need to kiss you more."

She nodded. "On that, I can agree completely, but roping isn't completely off the table either."

He let out his breath and smiled at her with love shining from his eyes. "I love you so much."

She looked for the doctor but he had disappeared. Louise turned back to Grayson with a slightly wicked grin. "Show me."

# ABOUT REINA TORRES

Reina reads like she writes-
- Heat to Sweet
- Contemporary to Historical
- Normal to Paranormal
- Military,
- First Responders
- & More
- Always with an HEA because we all deserve the same!

Made in the USA
Monee, IL
28 September 2024